DEATH AT SEA

THE SUMMIT GROUP

1227 West Magnolia, Suite 500 • Fort Worth, Texas 76104

94 95 96 97 98 99   5 4 3 2 1

ISBN 1-563530-165-X

Cover and book design by David Sims

DEATH at Sea

A Murder Mystery in 3-D

by LEN OSZUSTOWICZ

Illustrated by Brian Small

THE SUMMIT GROUP ● FORT WORTH, TEXAS

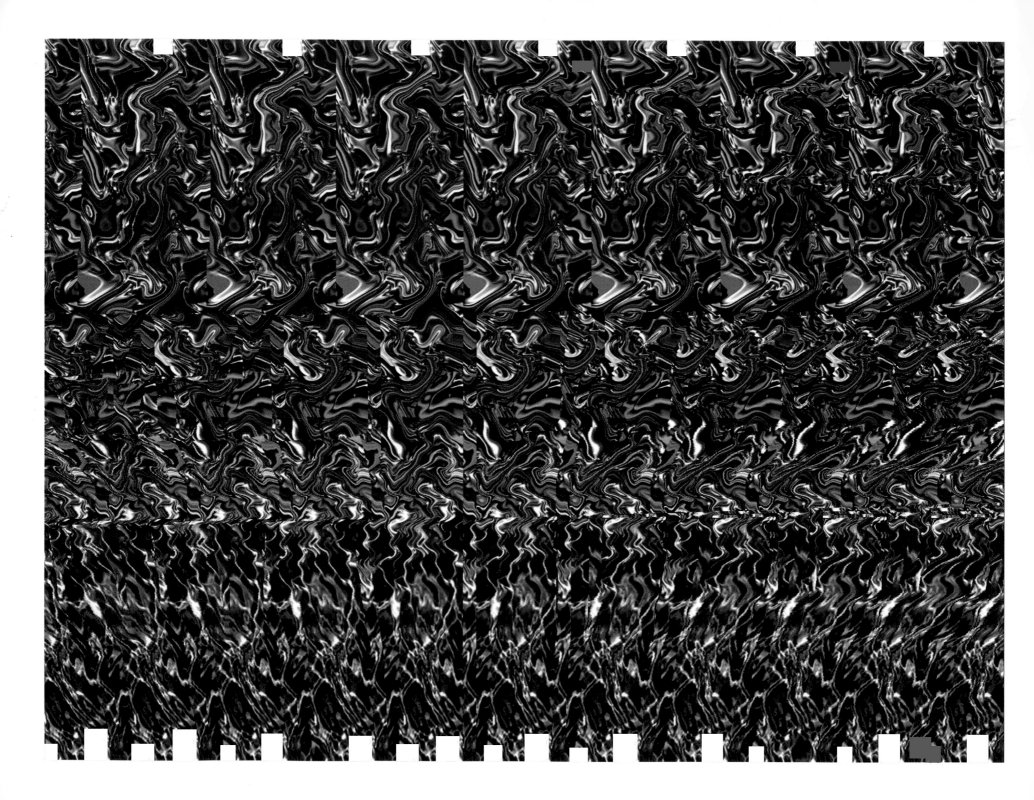

Chapter 1

H. Parkington Bowles was not one to tolerate foolishness. As a senior inspector with Scotland Yard, he normally escaped the drudgery of routine police work, such as filling out reports on bothersome souls who chose inconvenient places to die. Thirty-seven years on the job had earned him the privilege of dealing only with those cases involving the most heinous acts—murder, rape, mayhem—which challenge the wit and fascinate the souls of men who enjoy such work. So on this postcard London morning, he went through the motions of completing the sheaf of paperwork associated with the death of a seventy-two-year-old dowager named Millicent

Prestwood while awaiting the return of her ship, the *Queen's Speed*, to Dock 23 in London's East Harbor.

Queen's Speed Captain Harvey Clark had already radioed ahead to inform authorities that there had been a death on board while at sea. To every seaman, even the captain of a pleasure ship, maritime law is serious business, clearly dictating which actions had to be taken upon the determination that a life had been lost upon the high seas. Not surprisingly, therefore, a contingent of law enforcement personnel, led by Inspector Bowles, was on hand to greet the ship when she anchored in London.

Without fanfare, Bowles went aboard and took control. His ill humor was obvious as he climbed the companionway and brushed aside Captain Clark's formal attempt to greet the boarders like some naval captain from an old war movie. Bowles's was a mission of inconvenience and he made it clear that if he had to do this job, it would be done without the ridiculous affectations of a class of people he had very little time for in the first place.

In the gruff and direct style for which he was well known and feared, Bowles "greeted" the passengers on board the boat: "I'm sorry for your loss; however, it has been my experience that these things *do* happen to elderly people. As I'm certain your captain has told you, Scotland Yard will be required to implement an investigation. We are no more thrilled by this idea than you are; therefore, if you will cooperate, we can complete our work all the sooner."

With that greeting, Park Bowles turned and left the group of bewildered passengers and officials, and began the task of acquiring a basic understanding of what had taken place on board over the last three days. While instructing the passengers to stay put and make way for official personnel, he turned to his assistant of twelve years, Henry Colf, and barked, "Let's go see the dead lady who's going to waste the next two weeks of our lives."

If Bowles's manners had not alienated the passengers aboard the *Queen's Speed* by now, this comment surely did. The dumbfounded looks among the passengers made it clear that none of them had ever before dealt with a character like H. Parkington Bowles. As Bowles and Colf headed for Millicent Prestwood's cabin, it was already clear that this was going to be a most unpleasant experience for everyone involved.

As Bowles began his descent, he interrupted his ranting just long enough to call back to his assistant, "Colf, come in here and tell me who else was on this bloody boat!"

Obediently, Colf followed Bowles into the galley and in two minutes regurgitated his three hours of background research.

"There were six souls on board the *Queen's Speed* when she left the Port of London Friday, July 20, bound for a cruise of undetermined duration and destination," Colf started. "The dead woman is Millicent Prestwood, age seventy-two, widow of the late Sir Milton Prestwood, ex-chair of the Royal Bank of Britain and dozens of other commercial, charitable, and political concerns. She apparently died of heart failure sometime late Sunday night or early Monday morning. Her body was found at roughly 7:15 A.M. Monday by Dr. Jonas Steed, personal physician and family friend. No sign of foul play."

"Did she drink?" Bowles asked with characteristic tact.

"No record at this point," Colf responded.

"How about medication?"

Colf just shrugged.

"Who else?" Bowles asked impatiently.

"Bethany Ann Prestwood; daughter of the deceased. Age thirty-three. She's a looker, that one, Inspector. Great body, unmarried, but spoken for. Does very little, but live the life of leisure, and toy with charities and such when convenient. She's had drug problems in the past and drinks too much, although you couldn't tell it from her looks. Fairly intelligent, but quite naive. She was a daddy's girl, and since he's been gone she's been a mess. Blamed her mother for everything bad in the last thirty years, including famine in Africa and the decrease in the whale population. Seemingly in love with a gent who was also aboard," Colf reported, taking care to keep it brief and salient . . . he had worked with Bowles too long to do otherwise.

"You forgot to mention whether you noticed if she was attractive, Henry!" Bowles sarcastically taunted his young assistant while he scribbled furiously into the worn leather pad he compulsively carried. "Did Daddy leave his little girl with a bundle, or did she get her pin money from Mummy?"

Again, Colf shook his head as he had learned to do, and forged ahead with his presentation rather than give Bowles time to pepper him with minutiae. Continuing, Colf said, "The fella accompanying Bethany was her fiancé, Charles Collett. A lucky one he is, Inspector. A real dandy. Sharp dresser. No visible means of support. Mid-thirties and a real pretty boy. He's been courting Bethany on and off for a few years, and got on well with the late Mr. Prestwood. Sort of birds of a feather they were. The missus, though, hated him passionately and made no secret of it."

"He sounds like the embodiment of all that is wrong with the United Kingdom today," Bowles preached as he completed an entry in his pad with a wild flourish. "What other ne'er-do-wells were floating the high seas when the old girl cashed in her chips?"

Muffling a snicker, Colf continued his briefing. "Passenger number four was Dr. Jonas Steed, late sixties. Practitioner of internal medicine and chaser of dolly birds."

Now it was Bowles's turn to chuckle.

"Steed was a mate of the late Sir Milton Prestwood and has served as the family doctor to the Prestwoods for more than forty years," Colf said. "He is a widower who fills his days with golf and his nights with the high life."

"Passenger number five was Captain Harvey Clark. Captain Clark was a decorated officer in the

Royal Navy, in whose service he sustained grievous wounds on behalf of the queen. Upon his rehabilitation, he was retained by the Prestwood family to captain their vessel and see to its needs. A pretty cushy job that pays well and requires little time. When he's not piloting the upper crust of London society about the sea, he gambles a bit, as was his habit when Mr. Prestwood and he were running mates."

Colf seemed determined to speak at such a rate that Bowles would be forced to ask him to slow the pace of his delivery. Knowing Bowles as he did, however, Colf realized that Bowles would rather lose a finger than admit that he couldn't keep up.

So Colf continued, "Finally, Inspector, the only other passenger was Gerald Blume, the Prestwood family chef—"

Bowles interrupted: "Was it the doctor who found the body?" He asked not so much to get an answer, but to slow the rhythm of Colf's diatribe.

"I understand that it was, Inspector," Colf responded.

"Fine. You may continue, Henry," Bowles said impatiently as he turned the page.

"Well, Inspector, not really much else to say right now. Each of these folks appears to be a decent human being and legitimately sorry for the death of their friend," Colf finished, nearly out of breath.

"That's bloody good enough for now," the Inspector abruptly proclaimed. "Let's go and have a look at London's late, great society lady." And with that he pushed his way through the narrow door and past the young assistant, who never ceased to marvel at his boss's irreverence.

⎯⎯⎯✦⎯⎯⎯

After viewing the body, Bowles took a quick inventory of Millicent's shipmates, all of whom were milling about in what looked more like an *alfresco* cocktail party than the investigation of a death by Scotland Yard. But Bowles had known many such uncomfortable instances of meandering prattle by those forced by circumstances to converse, with very little to say.

Anxious to get started, he requested that all passengers join him on the deck, where he set about gathering a synopsis of the

events surrounding Mrs. Prestwood's death. Since the odds against foul play were overwhelming, Bowles decided that individual interviews were a waste of his time. While this was somewhat irregular, he was confident that no harm would come of it.

Following his plenary interview, in which he heard from each of the passengers a summary of their activities on Sunday evening, he requested that each remain available within the London environs for further reference. He then instructed them that they were free to leave the boat, which had by now been cordoned off and secured by his fellow agents of Scotland Yard. On hearing this instruction from Bowles, however, Colf quietly called him aside and reminded him of an archaic law of the sea.

Section 50 (b)(6) of the Maritime Code required that all "cargo" on the ship where a death at sea occurs must be quarantined and inspected, lest it is determined that some ghastly creature from another country caused the death. Reasonable for cargo ships, Bowles supposed, but ludicrous for an entertainment vessel such as this. Still, he was too tired and apathetic to fight it, so Bowles figured that he might just as well go ahead and enforce it.

As the passengers approached the gangway to leave the boat, Bowles announced, "I'm afraid that I am forced to inconvenience you once more. You see, you each may leave the boat, but your gear must stay aboard, where it will be quarantined, inspected, and returned to you shortly. Therefore, if you will place all your baggage in Captain Clark's cabin, you are free to go, after I have cataloged the personal effects you will be carrying off the boat."

"What the devil for?" asked a too-tired and ill-tempered Collett.

"It's just like the Yard," mocked Bethany, taking up for her fiancé. "They have to poke their noses into every corner. It makes them feel important."

Bowles had little tolerance for this type of juvenile banter and stared them down, stating squarely, "Irrespective of either your feelings about the law or mine, it is the law and we will comply with it. So be off now and stow your belongings."

Slowly, each of the passengers made off to do as the inspector had

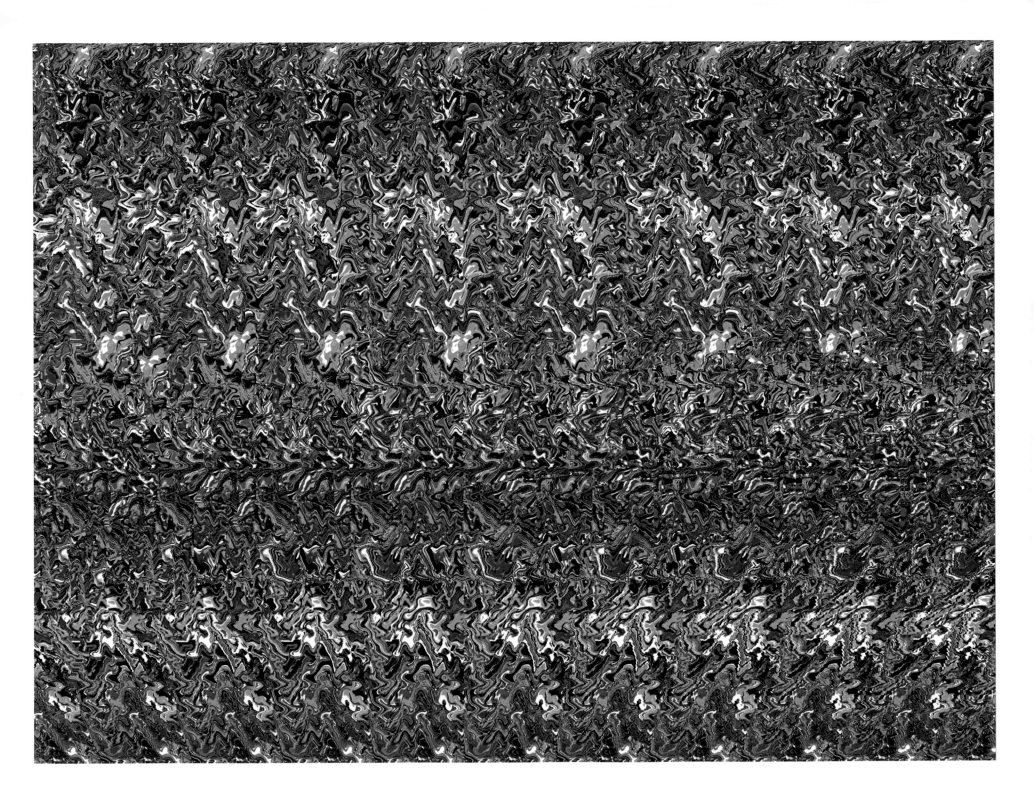

asked, with Bethany and Charles continuing their muttering as they walked.

<hr />

Before allowing them to disembark, Bowles searched each passenger and scribbled the following list into his ever-present leather pad:

Captain Harvey Clark

(departure time 10:34 A.M.)

1. One wallet, containing 76 pounds, 3 shillings, 12 pence
2. One standard issue Royal Navy pocketknife
3. One handkerchief, roughly 30 cm. x 30 cm.
4. One pair of reading glasses
5. One set of keys to a Peugeot, with various other keys attached

Bethany Ann Prestwood

(departure time 10:39 A.M.)

1. One bag (Vuitton) containing:
   a. One compact
   b. One wallet containing 356 pounds, 10 shillings, 35 pence
   c. One package of tissue
   d. One key to a Mercedes Benz (with other keys attached)
   e. One can of mace spray
   f. One roll of peppermint lozenges
   g. One pair of sunglasses (Vuarnet)
   h. One tube of lipstick (Passion Rose)
   i. One perfume spray (Opium)
   j. One theater ticket stub

Charles Collett

(departure time 10:45 A.M.)

1. One wallet containing 7 pounds
2. One pair of sunglasses (Bolle)
3. One key ring containing various keys

Chef Gerald Blume

(departure time 10:52 A.M.)

1. One medallion (St. Christopher)
2. One wallet containing 47 pounds
3. One Swiss Army knife
4. One shopping list for the market

Doctor Jonas Steed

(departure time 11:04 A.M.)

1. One wallet containing 134 pounds
2. One key fob holding 5 keys, one to a Jaguar
3. One liquor flask, silver
4. One pen (Waterman)
5. One pocket watch, gold
6. 11 business cards

After dismissing the passengers and tying up loose ends with his colleagues securing the boat, Bowles headed his dusty old Rover for The Blackmoor's Head Pub, a run-down venue that he frequented while in this end of town.

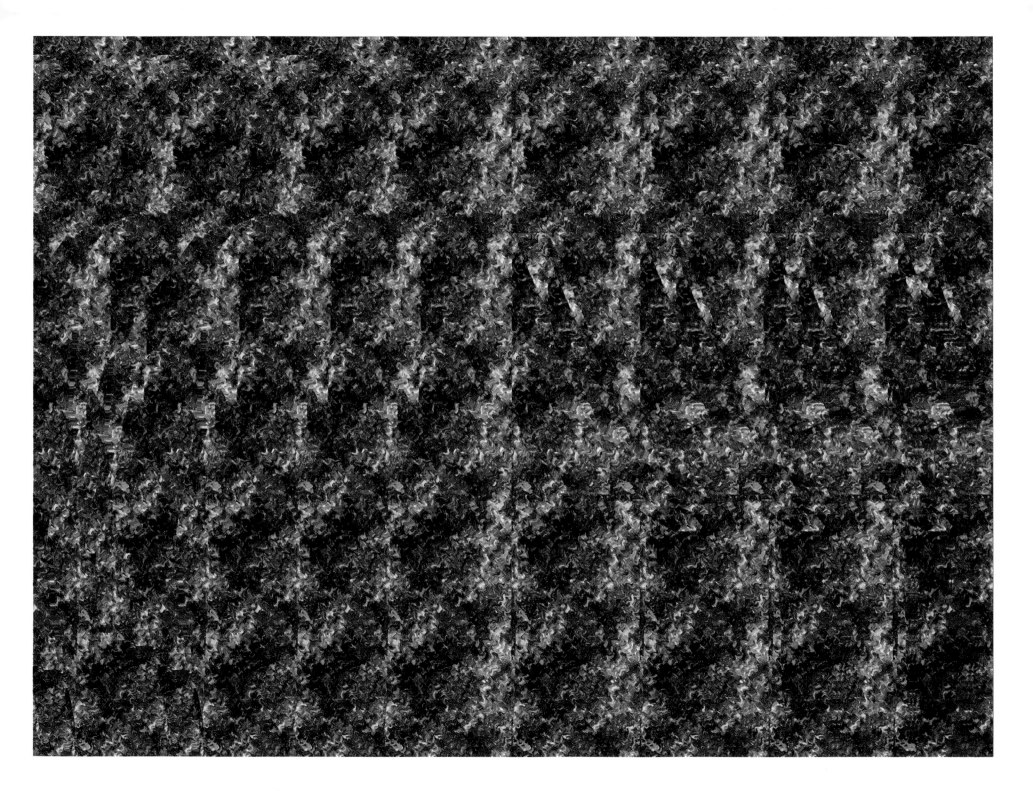

After enjoying a ploughman's lunch of bread, cheese, and delicious pickled onions—washed down with a pint of lager—he returned to his desk at Scotland Yard. There, his first order of business was to request Millicent Prestwood's medical records from the medical examiner, whose office would already have started gathering such data. Required by the Code to include their review in his report anyway, he took advantage of the opportunity to speak with Margaret Downes-Farrington, a fortyish redhead with hot blood and a warm heart. It was Margaret whose close professional and budding personal relationship with Bowles helped remind him that his flame, while flickering weakly, still at least flickered.

"Maggy!" blubbered a sophomoric Bowles. "Why haven't you called? I thought you had finally run off with one of your twenty-five-year-old studs!"

"Park, you old flirt, how nice to hear from you again. Is this my knight in shining armor coming to sweep me away, or are you just calling again to use my mind and leave my body alone?"

"Sadly, Maggy, today I need your mind and I must put off till another day the conquest of that great bod of yours."

"Same old Park Bowles. All business. Oh, well, what can I do for you today, you old lecher?" Margaret asked with mock irritation.

"Maggy, I need the medical records of one Millicent Prestwood," Bowles asked more seriously.

"You mean *the* Millicent Prestwood?"

"One and the same, Maggy. She bought it this morning, while boating throughout the Isles, and I got lucky enough to get to put together the maritime report. How soon can you get your beautiful hands on it and send it over?" Bowles inquired.

"Well, Park, for most people, I would say a couple of days; but for you, how about two weeks?" she kidded.

"Oh, thanks, luv," Bowles said, going along with her joke.

"No, seriously, I'll have to wait for the autopsy report, which, as you will recall, must be done in such cases."

Bowles knew this meant that he would have to mess with this case for several weeks, instead of a couple of days as he had hoped. Not disguising well his irritation, he said, "Well Maggy, if that's how long it takes for the bureaucrats to earn their money, then so be it."

Maggy Farrington recalled a day when Bowles's comment might have angered her, but those days were long past. She was one of the few who could see beneath the veil which so completely shielded the outside world from the real Herbert Parkington Bowles. She was one of the few who saw beneath the sarcasm and irreverence and understood the good, though tired soul surviving quietly beneath the surface.

There was no question that Park Bowles was an odd bird who lived his life against the grain. He not only failed to see the world the way others saw it, but he also simply didn't care how others viewed it. He was a man who made others ill at ease. His quirky ways alienated those who might have been friends. On the other hand, those were the same traits that made him the best inspector in the Yard: he took nothing at face value and believed that people were basically good—but that the mix of good to bad was at best about 52/48.

In fact, life had done little to prove Park Bowles's appraisal wrong. Nine years earlier, his wife, Anne, had been killed by a pipe bomb meant to take him out of a dope case he was working on. But even in light of Park's pain, Maggy knew better than to coddle him. She knew she was a balancing force in his life, and she played the role well.

"Park, I believe you're getting more cantankerous every day. I'll get it to you first, okay?" Maggy responded in a reassuring tone. "Do you think something unholy is up?"

"No. I'm only doing my sworn duty to the people and the Crown," Bowles stated theatrically. "Why?"

Margaret reported offhandedly as she buffed one of her blood red fingernails, "I saw her not a week ago at a ball for the widows and orphans of the Royal Air Force dancing the night away. Hardly on her last legs, but I guess when you get up in years, these things happen. Of course, I hardly need to tell you about the perils of old age!"

"Indeed you do! As a matter of fact, I would like it very much if you would explain them to me in detail over dinner one evening soon." Bowles asked conspiratorially, as if planning the overthrow of the monarch rather than asking for a date.

"When I get the reports, I'll explain them to you along with your questions of geriatrics," she said, dismissing Bowles lightly.

"I'll count the minutes, Maggy," he responded charmingly.

With that, Bowles set about organizing what he had learned so far, only to be suddenly interrupted by a call from the chief inspector of Scotland Yard, Miles Carrie, who claimed to have some interesting background material from a related case to share with him. With a well-muffled huff, Bowles agreed to meet Carrie the next morning at eleven to hear what he had to offer.

Meanwhile, it struck Bowles that if half of the free world was going to be looking over his shoulder, as much as he hated to admit it, he had better cross his t's and dot his i's. Therefore, he undertook to schedule personal interviews with each of the passengers who had been on board the *Queen's Speed*. When finished with that, he resumed the painstaking process of turning his jumbled notes into a proper report, a process he detested.

Chapter 2

ood morning, Miles," Bowles said, forcing an accommodating smile.

"Hi, Park. What do you have?"

"Well, Chief Inspector, there isn't much to tell. Millicent Prestwood, age seventy-two, sailed off with friends and crew for a few days of fresh air on board her yacht. While she was at it, she seems to have passed away in her sleep. There certainly doesn't seem to be anything out of order. However, we will know for certain when the medical examiner completes her report in a week or so. Until then, I'll cover the normal bases and, hopefully, tie this up quickly," Bowles explained matter-of-factly.

Inspector Carrie listened carefully. After a brief pause, he stated coldly, "Park, I'm concerned with how casually you're dismissing this matter. I don't need to remind you of the power of the Prestwood name. It has carried impact in the highest corridors of British government for decades. Now, then, why don't we discuss a few of the bits and pieces of this dreadful situation?"

Carrie continued, "I am told that Millicent despised the young man who is to wed her daughter, Bethany. What's his name . . . Collett, I believe? Our sources tell us that Millicent Prestwood had retained in her employ a private investigator to dig into Collett's comings and goings. We came across him while pursuing our own case concerning Collett's involvement in the drug trade. We know that Millicent had publicly pledged to do what she had to in order to see to it that Collett and Bethany never married. Probably just a convenient coincidence for Collett that the old girl died before she could do anything about it. However, you might want to buckle down and see what you can find."

Bowles, suppressing his bile, asked impatiently, "Well, *Chief* Inspector, what other morsels have you collected from your society snoops?"

"I was confident that you could put business ahead of your ego, Park, but it seems obvious you can't. Look, I know it's been a tough year since I was chosen chief inspector at your expense. But we're too old and too good at what we do to let pride come between us at this late date. I truly am sorry that one of us had to be passed over, but I can't help that anymore. We've been like brothers for over thirty years and saved each other's lives more times than we can count. It's time to get on with life, Park, because in case you haven't noticed, it's not waiting for you," Carrie said in a friendly tone.

"Geez, Miles, I'm sorry. I guess I'm just an old warhorse who thinks his time is better spent catching *real* boogeymen than making sure that every Society Sal's reputation is protected in death as well as in life," Bowles said, still wounded.

"Park, you're the best inspector in the Yard—you wouldn't be on this case if we didn't have reasons to stir the porridge a bit. In addition to Collett's situation, you might find it interesting that Millicent Prestwood had been carrying on socially with her physician. Not to mention there are those who can't quite figure out the deal between Millicent and her sailor friend, Harvey Clark. Anyway, Park, these are all things you would have uncovered soon, if you haven't already. I thought I could save you some time by filling you in on what our other agents in the field have sniffed out."

"Thanks for the consideration. Is that all?" Bowles asked, more than slightly miffed by being scooped.

"One other thing, Park. The media will swarm onto this case in the worst way, whether Mrs. Prestwood's death was innocent or not. Let's cover our bases and see to it that we aren't embarrassed."

"Sure thing," spat Bowles.

Carrie shrugged. "Remember, Park, we're all on the same team."

With that, Bowles retreated from Carrie's office to the nearest pub, where his ego and his headache both found relief from their anguish in the twelve-year-old Chivas that, in his mind, was the crowning glory of the British Commonwealth.

Chapter 3

The next morning arrived well ahead of schedule for Parkington Bowles as his efforts to drown his pain the evening before demanded repayment the morning after. Nonetheless, he set about the task of righting himself for the interviews he had scheduled this day by downing a mixture of eggs, tomato juice, and bitters to settle his stomach. He realized that the value of the horrid mixture was not so much in its medicinal properties, but in its psychological properties—having to face this terrible elixir might cause him to think twice before turning to a bottle for his therapy next time.

First on the list for the morning was a meeting with Dr. Jonas Steed, Millicent's personal physician and the one who found her body.

"Well, Dr. Steed, first of all, please allow me to express my sympathy. Unfortunately, the law requires me to make a full report, so I am compelled to ask you to explain to me the events as you know them surrounding the death of Millicent Prestwood," Bowles began as he tentatively proceeded with his perfunctory investigation.

Steed outlined for Bowles the sequence of events surrounding his visit to Millicent's cabin at roughly 7:15 A.M. It was to provide her morning medication, at which time he found the body.

"Millicent had been quite ill in recent months, resulting in part from the trauma of her husband's

death," he said in a distant monotone.

"While she seemed to have regained some of her physical health, she was hurting mentally. Frankly, I believe that much of her illness was in her old, gray head. In fact, my very presence on this trip was more in the role of a friend and counselor, and less as a medical doctor. The poor girl just died of a broken heart."

"Of course," he continued, "she had been greatly upset with Bethany's personal life lately, and that undoubtedly put additional strain on her."

"Please explain, Doctor," Bowles implored, a spark of interest in his tone.

"Well, it was obvious that Millicent did not approve of the lifestyle of her soon-to-be son-in-law. And for good reason. She knew that he ran with a bad crowd, and Millicent simply didn't want to see her only daughter hurt. That's what Millicent and Collett were shouting about on the night before her death."

Bowles edged closer. "Tell me about this shouting match."

"We all heard it. Millicent and Collett were outside her cabin after dinner, when they began to yell at one another. At one point I heard Collett tell her that he loved her daughter and that there was nothing Millicent could do to stop them from getting married. To which she shouted, 'Perhaps not, but I can take away the gold at the end of your rainbow, you cheap hoodlum. When I finally prove to Bethany what kind of scum you are I won't have to stop you—she'll drop you cold.' "

"How did Collett respond, Doctor?"

"To the best of my knowledge, he didn't," Steed said pensively. "I heard not another sound from him after that."

"Why do you say that 'everyone could hear'?" Bowles inquired.

"Quite simple, my good man. Initially, maybe some couldn't. But by the time the tempest boiled over, we had all gathered on deck to eavesdrop. Millicent was so shaken that she retired to her cabin where she and Captain Clark shared a brandy."

"Doctor, is it your business to chronicle everyone's movements so carefully?" Bowles probed, expecting to be chastened by a venomous response from the doctor.

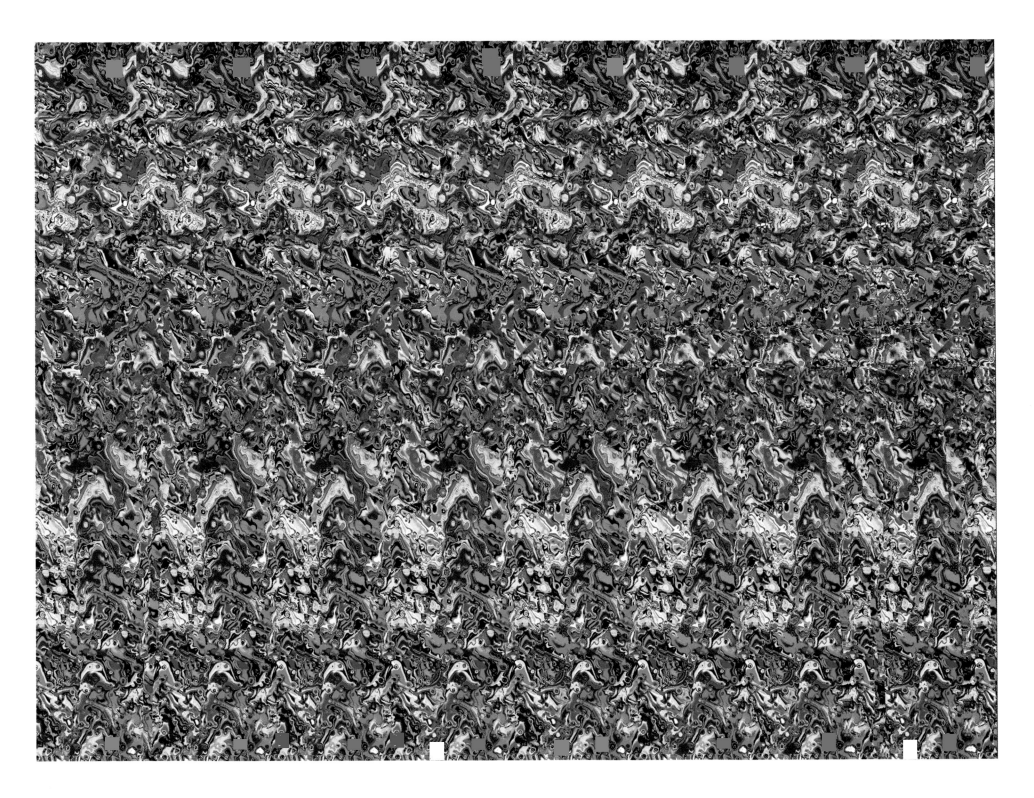

Steed demurred and instead continued his story with clinical precision. "I am aware of the *tête-à-tête* between Clark and Millicent, only because Clark called me to her cabin shortly before 10:00 P.M. to administer Millicent's heart medication. He indicated that she was extremely shaken by the confrontation with Collett and had vowed to put the young money grabber in his place upon her return to London. In any event, I administered a quarter-milligram of Drimatosin and left her in the company of the Captain."

"Then Clark was the last one to see her alive?" Bowles asked.

"How in blazes should I know, Inspector? That is your job, not mine. I only know that the poor lady was seriously shaken when I left her."

Feeling that he had sufficiently covered the relevant issues, Bowles bade his good-byes, adding as he dismissed Steed, "Doctor, was Mrs. Prestwood's health so weak that such a confrontation could cause her death . . . in your opinion?"

"It did. Didn't it, Inspector?"

With that, Dr. Jonas Steed tipped his hat and briskly proceeded to the third-floor corridor leading away from the musty closet that served as Bowles's office.

———⊲⊳●⊂———

Upon Steed's departure, Bowles rang up Captain Harvey Clark and asked him to courier over a copy of the layout of the *Queen's Speed* along with a map of the route she took on her most recent voyage.

Something that Steed had said struck him as odd, so he figured he might just as well use the blueprint to provide some perspective to the flow of events.

His next call was to Trevor Moss, the solicitor who had handled Prestwood affairs for years. Bowles arranged to stop by the next day to pick up a copy of the last testaments of both Mr. and Mrs. Prestwood. Bowles realized that he was being drawn into a deeper investigation than he had planned; he wasn't sure whether it was his cynical nature or legitimate concerns that lured him beneath the surface of the seemingly calm waters of Millicent Prestwood's death.

He spent the balance of the day contemplating first his headache and second, the new developments of the case. In time, the incessant pain in his head won out and he returned to his flat where he at once fell into bed, wingtips and all.

———⊰✦⊱———

The following day started more favorably. Properly rested, Bowles felt compelled to move ahead in light of the mounting pressure for a final investigation report. He placed his first call to Harvey Clark and requested that he come by his office later that day to go over a few details. Clark agreed and volunteered to bring the layout of the *Queen's Speed* with him.

While waiting for Clark's arrival, Bowles sent Colf out for a tongue sandwich, some crisps, and pickled onions, which he figured would keep him going a few more hours. While enjoying this repast at his gray, metal, single-pedestal desk, Bowles browsed through the most recent news reports of the death of Millicent Prestwood, which had her dying of everything from the throes of passion with a twenty-three-year-old male prostitute, to her suicide resulting from her involvement with an international spy ring. Bowles imagined that the truth was somewhat less spectacular than all that, although he was beginning to believe that it wasn't as simple as a heart attack.

———⊰✦⊱———

Captain Harold William Clark's ship had literally come in through his association with the Prestwood family. For more than ten years he had stood at their beck and call to transport them and their guests about the Isles. Seldom did the task consume more than a few days in the average month, leaving him free to pursue his second favorite pastime, betting the ponies at Hertfordshire. His healthy stipend provided plenty of fuel for the captain to exercise his vice, and his recent squiring of Millicent Prestwood had seen to it that he was treated like royalty at the finest racing venues throughout the Commonwealth. It was a fortunate thing for Clark, too, that he had influential friends. His luck at the sport of kings had been all bad as of late, and there were many who were becoming concerned regarding the substantial sums Clark owed in and around the betting houses of London.

Around 2:30, Captain Clark was led into Bowles's office by Henry Colf, who seated himself on the low threadbare hassock beside Bowles's

Spartan desk. Fully attired in his Royal Navy uniform, Clark looked more like a returning war hero than the skipper of an old lady's yacht. His flowing silver hair, meticulously shorn beard, and swarthy tan imbued him with an air of wisdom and aristocracy—a man to be reckoned with. Added to his heavy bass voice, the captain presented quite a package.

"Good day, Captain," began Bowles. "Thanks for coming by."

"And a very good day to you, Inspector. Am I to gather from your request to speak with me that you have not yet rendered your final report on Millicent's death?" Clark intoned, without frivolity.

"Well frankly, Captain, this is all just routine. Have you brought along the route map?"

Unfolding the map as if it were a guide to buried treasure, Clark launched into a long-winded explanation of the course of the *Queen's Speed*.

"I see, sir, that there are two sets of lines on this map. One line runs its course until it eventually is split in two. What is their significance?" Bowles asked as he traced the lines on a thin sheet produced from a tablet of onion skin.

"This first line represents the original planned course of the ship. The point where the line splits indicates a course change, which was called for by Mrs. Prestwood on the night before her death."

Bowles asked intently, "When was this new course laid in?"

Reflecting deeply (too deeply, Bowles thought), Clark recited, "After dinner, young Collett had a

row with Millicent, and shortly thereafter I received a call on the intercom from Millicent asking me to come by her cabin. I did so without delay and was greeted at the door by an extremely angry lady. She demanded to know at once where we were and how long it would take to return to London. When I told her I would have to check our maps, she instructed me to do so immediately and to make full speed toward London. I said that I would do so at once. However, as I turned to leave, she asked me to summon Dr. Steed so that he could administer her heart medication and a little something to calm her stomach."

"Did Dr. Steed do as she asked?" inquired Bowles.

"I really don't know, Inspector. I presume he did. I went about my

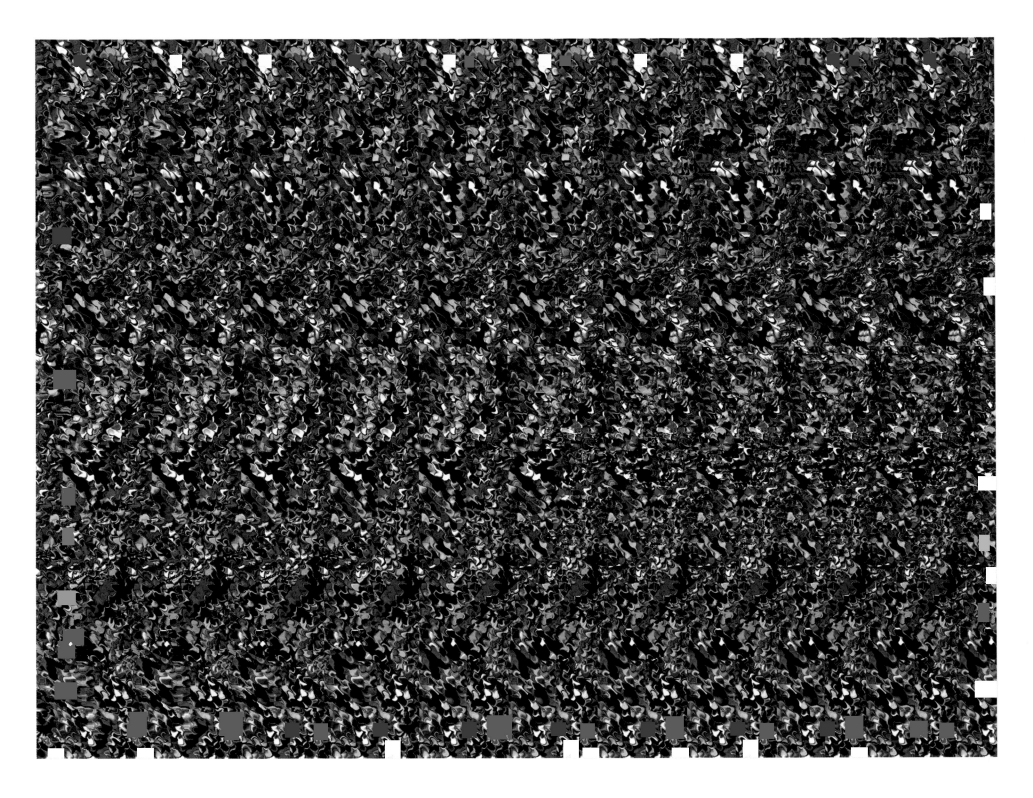

business and didn't speak with him again that night."

"Did you call her to confirm your heading and expected time of arrival in London?" Bowles asked.

"No, I did not. However, on my way to my cabin later that night—oh, probably about eleven—I decided to stop by her quarters and fill her in on my findings. As I approached her door, though, I heard loud crying coming from inside. So I decided against bothering Millicent and her daughter, whose name I heard spoken over the sobs. Not wishing to interfere, I turned and headed for my cabin and a good night's sleep."

Bowles looked confused, "If you were retiring for the evening, who was piloting the ship?"

"Oh, I *am* sorry, Inspector. Did I not mention to you that Charles Collett is a registered boatman whose presence on the trip was as a seaman as well as a guest? No matter. Collett might be a first-rate ass, but he's also a first-rate sailor. I gave him the new heading and he took the night watch at the helm."

"Then he was aware of the course change?" Bowles asked rhetorically.

"Of course," responded Clark.

"To what did you attribute the changes to your itinerary when you briefed Collett?" Bowles asked.

"He knew bloody well why we were heading back to London. As he said it, 'The old crow can't wait to get back to town to see to it that I never so much as smell any Prestwood money, let alone spend any.' He knew he was plotting a course that would lead him away from his goal of marrying Bethany," Clark offered.

Bowles at once shifted the conversation by asking about his relationship with Millicent Prestwood.

"I understand, Captain, that you and Millicent had been keeping company. Is that true?"

Clark stiffened noticeably as he gazed squarely into the inspector's eyes. "Yes, Inspector. Millicent was a wonderful woman with whom I believe I was falling in love."

Hearing this bit of information somehow shocked Bowles, even though he was already aware that some relationship existed.

"You see, Inspector, Millicent was an exceptional woman. After the death of her husband, she sought comfort. But what did she get from that horrid daughter of

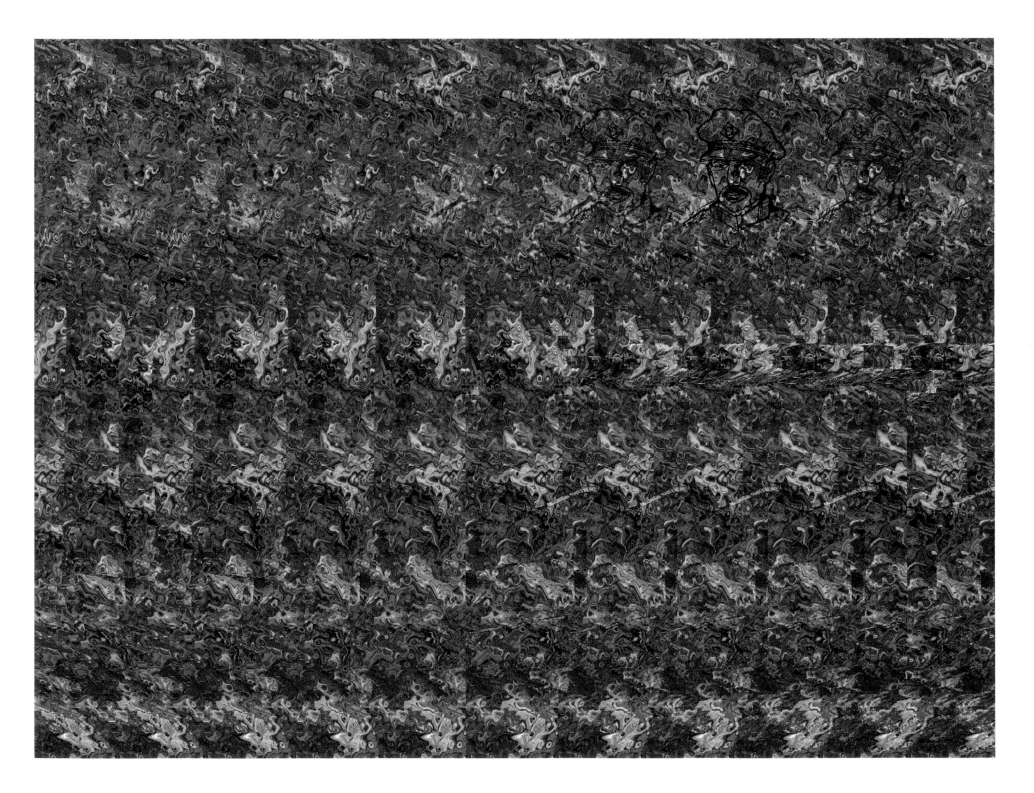

hers? From her only child? Nothing but grief. Bethany refused to let go of this Collett character in spite of Millicent's strong protests."

Bowles responded, "Sounds to me as though Bethany is really in love. Isn't that the way all children respond when their parents tell them what to do? That only stiffened Bethany's resolve to be with Collett."

"Well, Bethany may or may not be in love with Collett. One can never tell with a girl like her—up today, down tomorrow. Only one thing was constant in her life, and that was the blame she poured on her mother over the death of her father. Bethany believed that Millicent forced him to maintain a social schedule that far out-stretched his health, all for the sake of her position in society. Simply put, Inspector, Bethany hated her mother," Clark announced, his face taking on a bright red glow that oddly seemed to clash with his ornate uniform.

"Please forgive me, Inspector, I'm rambling."

"No, please continue," Bowles assured him.

"In any case, Inspector, I *did* begin to keep company with Millicent and we accepted each other for what we are. She was a sad and lonely old lady, and I was a broken-down sailor," related the captain.

"Just so," remarked Bowles, whose mind flashed back to the fact that Captain Harvey Clark was not only a broken-down sailor, but a "broke" sailor as well—one whose bad luck at the horse track had outlasted his money supply. Bowles wondered whether Millicent's will might include enough of a bequest to Captain Clark that might make her worth more to the good captain dead than alive.

Bowles followed up, "Captain, I was of the understanding that Mrs. Prestwood and Dr. Steed were very close. Was he not of comfort to her?"

"Yes, he was. Since Milton Prestwood died, Dr. Steed has been a constant companion. He spends a great deal of time at the Prestwood home and, in truth, has been a daily companion for both Millicent and Bethany. He is a good man. But his relationship with Mr. Prestwood made him unable to forge the sort of personal relationship with Millicent that she needed. I was able to supply that portion of her need. Besides, Dr. Steed's tastes run to a younger vintage of lady than Millicent."

"I see," said Bowles. "You've mentioned Bethany. What was her relationship with Dr. Steed?"

Clark explained, "He was Bethany's godfather. He watched her grow up. When Milton died, he became her surrogate father, and they grew closer. They spent time together and, in my opinion, he has been good for her. As wild as she is most of the time, when around him she seems to be a much calmer young lady."

"Finally, Captain, tell me about the chef on board, Mr.—uh—Mr. Blume. Gerald Blume."

"Inspector, Gerald is a fine sort. He and I have worked for the Prestwoods for many years. And they have taken very good care of him. The man is a master chef, and there was a perfect fit between the Prestwood family and Gerald. He served them outstanding cuisine and they took care of him. Sadly, the only thing lighter than Gerald's *soufflé* is his brain. The poor man is rather dull, begging your pardon."

Bowles was amused at the gentle way in which Clark spoke the truth about his old friend. "I understand," he said with a slight smile.

"Well, Captain, I don't suppose that I need to waste any more of your time. Thank you for your kindness in coming down to speak with me," Bowles said, extending his hand as he showed Clark the door.

"There is one question I would like to ask before I leave, if I may, Inspector," Clark asked tentatively. "Is there a suspicion of foul play?"

"No, sir, Captain, there is not. Unfortunately, as you well know, death at sea raises many questions and is governed by Maritime Law, under which an investigation of even the most straightforward cases is required," Bowles explained. "Have you any such suspicion, Captain?"

With a glare that would melt ice, Clark stated, "I would put nothing past Collett." And with that, he turned and left the office.

Chapter 4

Weekends had always been a special time for Park Bowles. As a young man, his weekends had represented freedom from the travails of work. When he was a father, they had represented the chance to spend time with his family and re-cement the bonds that were so weakened by his long hours during the week. Now though, with his wife gone and the children far away, Park Bowles found new fulfillment in the quiet times of weekends. He now used this time to catch up on his cases and to think through what had happened during the swirl of the prior week.

Sitting quietly in his study, Bowles began to create the report that would finally allow both Millicent Prestwood and the Maritime Board to be at rest. But even as he typed, he felt ill at ease. He pulled out a yellow tablet of paper to make a list of things that just didn't seem to jell.

Before he could write a word his phone rang.

"Park. Maggy. Hey, what's up, sport?"

"Maggy, you lovely creature, how are you? You must be clairvoyant. I have been sitting here pining for you all afternoon counting the minutes until we can be together," he groveled.

"Counting the minutes until I tell you about Millicent Prestwood's autopsy, you mean," she countered.

"Not so," came his response, dripping with offense. "That silly old report means nothing to me compared to you. But while we're at it, my lamb, what's the scoop?"

"Well, Park. Sorry to ruin your weekend, but Mili was poisoned."

"Is that true, Maggy?" Bowles asked, although she was only confirming a suspicion that had been growing in his mind for several days.

"Yessir. She certainly did have a heart attack. But it wasn't of her own making. I must admit that I missed it the first time through because the poison used—chlorol nitrate—causes damage very similar to a natural heart attack. But it just didn't sit straight with me . . . having seen her dance the night away so recently and then thinking of her dying of a heart attack while lazing on her yacht. It just didn't add up. So I did a few secondary tests and, *voilà*, there it was. Not much of it, but enough."

Bowles regained his composure and began carefully taking notes in his little red notebook. "Margaret, tell me. Is this chemical difficult to come by? Where might it have been

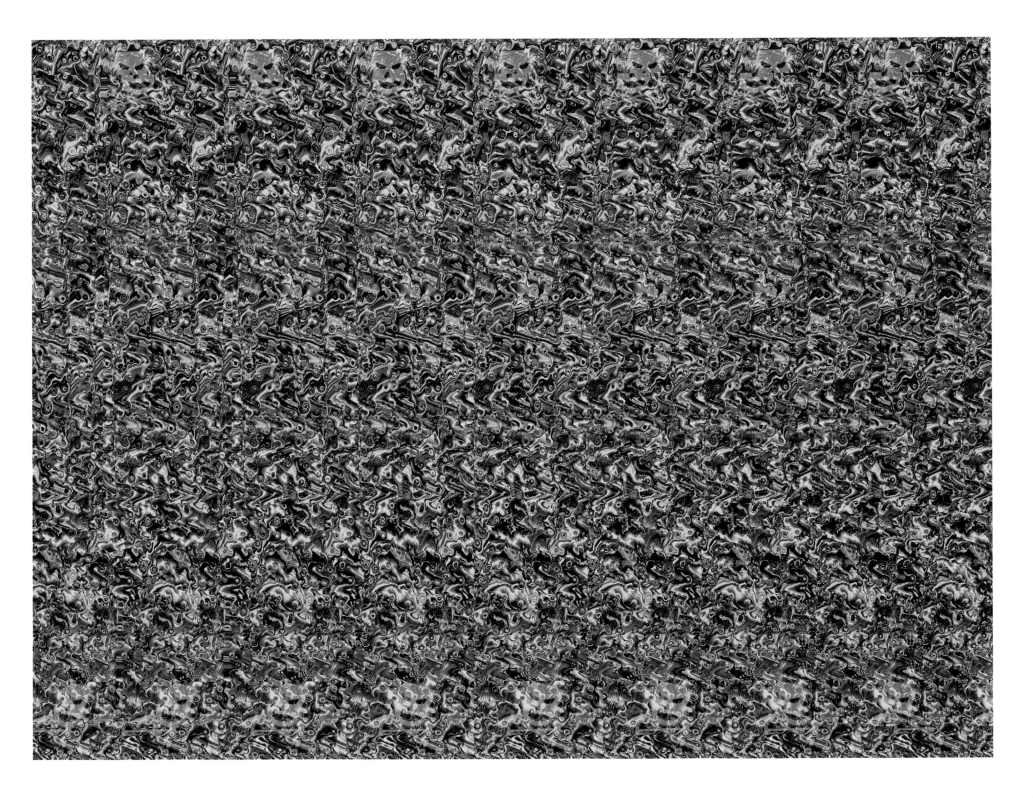

obtained and who would have access to it?"

Scoffing, Maggy answered, "That's the rub, Park. The stuff that caused her death is not hard to come by. Anyone could have gotten ahold of it. By itself, it causes few problems. But when it's taken with the Drimatosin she took for her heart . . . Whammo! A nearly silent killer."

"Is there a chance she took it in combination by mistake, Maggy?"

She answered patiently, "Not very likely, Park. She was an intelligent woman. She surely knew better than to ingest various and sundry chemicals on top of the medications she was already using. I think it's more likely that somebody fed it to her knowing that it might never be detected."

"If somebody knew her heart medication, could they have asked around and learned what the side effects of the combination of the two drugs would be?" he asked hopefully.

"Any doctor, pharmacist, chemist, or the like would know the danger of combining those drugs. Anyone else able to read and understand a doctor's reference book could also ascertain the danger, as could anyone versed in advanced first aid techniques. I guess what I'm saying, Park, is that this wasn't cold fusion. Almost anyone could have come up with this fatal combination."

"How about suicide?" Bowles asked.

"Park, if she was going to kill herself, there are a thousand less painful ways to end it. This was not

a pleasant death, believe me. In any event, I'll send over a copy of the report to you right now if you like," she offered.

"Only if you're the courier, Maggy," Bowles responded. "I've got a million more questions and no dinner plans."

Maggy loved the attention and her blush was almost visible over the telephone. "Just the report, dinner, and nothing more; do you understand, Park?"

"Just the report, dinner, and lots more," he promised.

Chapter 5

Upon his return to life on Sunday afternoon, Park Bowles swore a firm oath that he would never again carry on like a thirty-year-old. (It was a vow he had made and broken many times before.) As he regained his strength, eyesight, and energy, he pictured himself sitting alone and still half drunk, surrounded by the swirling reality that an innocent woman had been murdered. He tried hopelessly to begin to sort out the clues, motives, and methods. Unfortunately, his mind was not capable of this at this time. So in total surrender, he fell back into bed.

Monday morning was far more gracious to him than he deserved. The summer morning was glorious as the sunlight beamed into his room. But the glow of a beautiful morning was quickly eclipsed by the thought of Millicent Prestwood's murder flashing back into his mind. Suddenly, he returned to the dark side after his all-too-brief glimpse at the lighter side of life.

Nevertheless, he was now working on a murder case, and that was just the potion that revved H. Parkington Bowles back to life.

He reviewed in his mind the interviews of the past week and committed himself to reinspecting each of them in fine detail in light of the revelation from the coroner's report. As he scanned the morning papers, it became clear that each and every journalist in Great Britain had a theory for Millicent's death. Fortunately, he had been able to convince Maggy and the others to keep silent and stay with the party line that Prestwood's death was purely natural. But he had been in business too long not to realize that info that hot couldn't be kept secret for long.

He hoped that he could keep his secret until he completed his probe of the three remaining boat passengers. But now the game had changed.

His mind wandered as he realized that one of those to whom he had spoken was a cool liar, not to mention, of course, a cold-blooded murderer.

In light of the revelation of the poison, Bowles phoned Colf and instructed his assistant to go through the belongings of each passenger on board the *Queen's Speed*. Colf was then to submit all relevant items to the lab, where they could be searched for signs of chlorol nitrate. He knew that even if traces of the chemical were found, it wouldn't be a definitive answer, but it would certainly put pressure on somebody.

Whatever the case, Bowles had made an appointment for 8:00 A.M. with Chief Inspector Carrie to go over progress to date—a meeting which Bowles dreaded.

———⋙⋘———

Upon his arrival at Chief Inspector Carrie's office, Bowles was formally introduced to Trevor Moss, the Prestwoods' personal solicitor. Bowles was at first confused, but quickly figured that the presence of a dead woman's lawyer would soon enough be explained.

Bowles took the initiative. "It certainly does appear that the waters have become a bit murky since our last talk, Miles. What's the world coming to? It used to be that good people could go to sleep at night and be safe. It doesn't appear that one is safe even among a few 'trusted' friends anymore."

"It all depends on whom you trust," shot back Carrie. "So, Park, who dunnit?"

Bowles couldn't resist a light laugh as he acknowledged that his old friend still knew how to get to him. "Miles, I have a few ideas. I think I have it narrowed down to a list of about five. Pretty good work in such a short time, if you ask me.

"Seriously," Bowles continued, "I had my suspicions even before I got the coroner's report, but I had hoped that they would not be proven true. I suppose it's back to the drawing board. But while I'm here, what info have you dredged up?"

"Not a lot, Park. But what we've got is mighty interesting," Carrie enthusiastically said.

"Let's have it, Miles."

"We have it on a pretty firm basis that Charles Collett is bad news; however, it is widely believed that he was playing it straight with Bethany. Those who know them say that he wants to marry her in the worst way, with or without her mother's blessing," Carrie explained.

"I don't blame him. Nothing like a few million pounds' inheritance to strengthen one's resolve," Bowles charged.

"For good or bad, though, Park, it doesn't appear that Collett really needed the old girl's money. He might have what he has because he's a scoundrel, but it appears he's got plenty."

"Not likely, Miles. I know the type. The next pound is the most important pound. Once a man is hooked on money, it becomes a game. How he gets it is irrelevant . . . drugs, the rackets, pathetic young heiresses. It's all the same to these vultures. You know the type as well as I do, Miles. What else do you have?"

Miles Carrie enjoyed the back and forth with Bowles. It reminded him of his days back on the streets, when he was still doing *real* detective work. He added, "We did some background work on the rest of Millicent's friends and didn't find much. A couple of times, Bethany had been admitted into drug rehab clinics, but has apparently been clean for a few years. At least she hasn't been readmitted. Other than that and a smart-aleck mouth, she is a fairly normal rich kid. She grew up in the upper crust of London and has established herself as a de-cent member of society. She has worked intermittently in charitable causes and fancies herself to be a woman of substance.

Bowles scribbled feverishly as he listened. This was no longer an absurd exercise. A murderer was loose and that was enough to shake Bowles out of his malaise.

After pausing for a moment to allow Bowles to catch up, Carrie continued. "Let's see . . . the chef, Blume. He's a half-wit. Not a bad fella, really, but a bit slow. He and the captain are thick as thieves and have been through a few scrapes. But nothing serious. The only interesting thing there, is that he hangs around Bethany in a kind of puppy dog way. She feels sorry for him, but keeps him at arm's length. He's harmless, but to him she's the greatest."

Bowles followed up, "The one that I don't understand is this Clark character. Works a few days a month, gambles the rest. Falls in love with Millicent and now seems to be left out in the cold. The last thing he would have wanted was to have the old lady die if his plan was to get his hooks into the Prestwood purse."

"Not so fast," interrupted Trevor Moss, thrilled at the excitement of being out of probate court and into a real homicide investigation. "Harvey Clark, sea captain, stands to receive one hundred thousand pounds under the terms of Millicent Prestwood's will. That's a substantial sum, is it not? Enough to kill for, I might suspect."

"Possibly so," Bowles conceded, choking back a comment on the amateurish sleuthing attempted by this legal version of a bookkeeper.

"However, do we know that he was aware of his inheritance? When was that bequest added to her will—before or after the inception of their passion for one another?"

"Actually, that specific bequest flowed over from Mr. Prestwood's will. Millicent had no say in its creation," the barrister recited in his most officious tone, realizing for the first time that Bowles had already thoroughly reviewed both wills and was enjoying making him look foolish.

"What about Dr. Jonas Steed?" Bowles inquired, suddenly aware of the growing ire in the young lawyer's gaze.

Carrie responded, "To the best of our knowledge, Steed is what he appears to be; clean as a whistle, and dedicated to Millicent and her family. Quite wealthy in his own right, I might add. He took up the slack when Milton Prestwood died and has been an invaluable crutch to the family ever since."

Bowles couldn't resist the chance to take the offensive. "Yes, it does seem that each of these bastions of society is beyond reproach. Unfortunately, one of them killed a woman. If you have nothing more here, I'll be on my way to find out which one."

"Not so fast, Park," Carrie commanded. "I invited Moss here to tell us what transpired concerning Millicent's will on the night before her death. Trevor . . ."

Relishing the spotlight and the opportunity to prove that he wasn't a lightweight, Moss proceeded. "On the night before the passing of Millicent Prestwood, I was at my flat in Whipsnade recovering from an extremely challenging day, when I received a phone call on ship-to-shore radio from the *Queen's Speed*. The instructions I received from Captain Clark indicated that I was to meet Millicent Prestwood, Bethany Prestwood, and Charles Collett at her estate on the following evening at 8:00 P.M. I asked to know the issues to be discussed and was told, 'Just be there.' I agreed and went to bed. The next morning I was told that Millicent had died."

"Tell me, Mr. Moss, why do you suppose Mrs. Prestwood wanted to see you?" asked Carrie.

"I have no idea. The call was brief and I was tired," he answered.

Carrie continued, "And what matters did your firm handle for Mrs. Prestwood?"

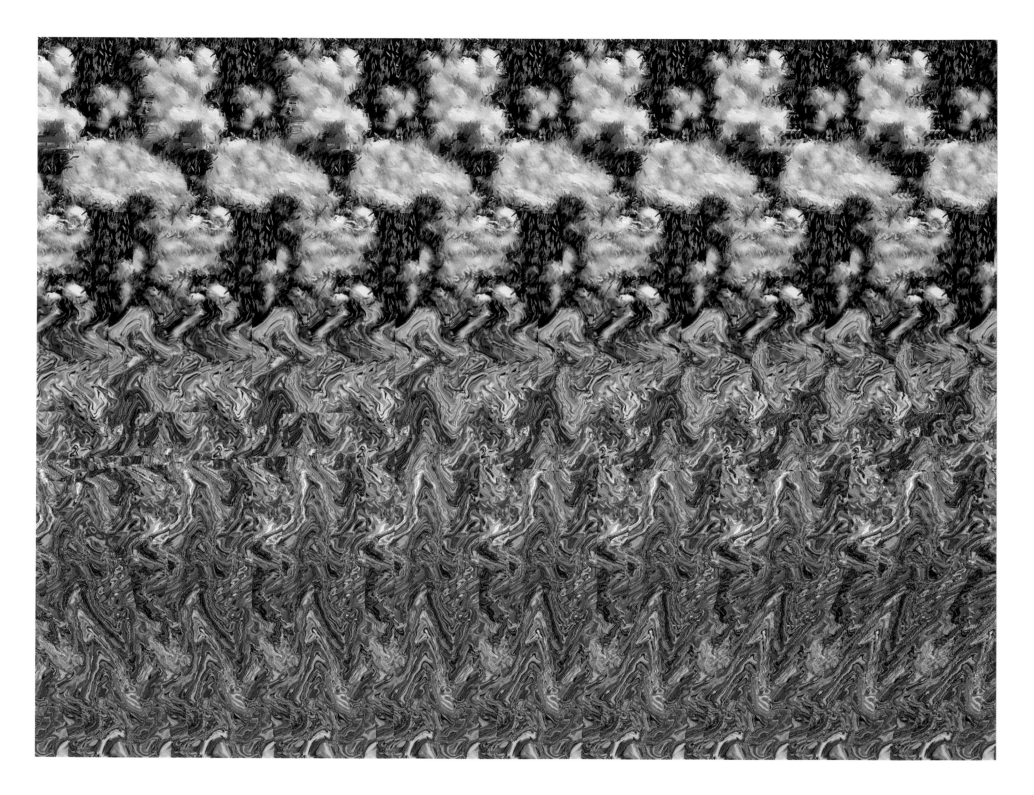

"All matters, I suppose," Moss said in a ponderous tone.

"So the call was not necessarily about a change to the will, correct, sir?" Bowles shot in. "She might well have been calling about any number of other matters. For example—your hiring a private investigator on behalf of Mrs. Prestwood?"

Moss was nonplused. Helplessly, he attempted to avoid the eyes of the inspectors, but their combined eighty years' experience knew at once that a lie was in the works. "She engaged our firm for many purposes, sir, but the specific nature of our services are protected by the privilege between a barrister and his client."

"In other words, *yes!*" blurted Bowles, sick of the slippery tongue of the solicitor. "You hired a private investigator to come up with dirt on Collett on her behalf so that anything he found out would be protected by privilege, didn't you? And she and you were going to seal Collett's doom with Bethany by spilling your guts out about your findings. Right?"

"Once again, sir, I regret to inform you that I am unable to speak to you about such things," Moss babbled, the sweat now rolling down his forehead in streams.

"That's fine, sir. However, I can assure you that Scotland Yard will not allow important information to be hidden from view without compelling reason. I hope that you and your firm are willing to live with the consequences of your lack of cooperation. Many will be dissatisfied, both in the Yard and all across London. Besides, your client is dead. The last thing she needs is attorney/client privilege!" Carrie shouted, the veins bulging from his neck like gorged snakes crawling from shoulder to head through a too-tight collar.

"We shall see, Chief Inspector, but I can assure you that our firm stands ready to be of whatever assistance we can, *within the law*," the barrister hissed.

"Thank you for your time, Mr. Moss. We shall speak again soon, I can assure you of that," Carrie goaded, dismissing the solicitor with a weak wave of his hand.

———◆———

"The world is being run by these idiots, Miles, and we can't do anything to take it back," Bowles said miserably.

"Don't be so sure, Park. They're still citizens of London, and London is our home field. In any event, let me take care of Moss. What else do you have? I've got another appointment in a couple of minutes," Carrie said apologetically.

"Not really much more for now. Thanks for the info." And with that Bowles departed the executive wing of the building, anxious to return to the familiar confines of the part of Scotland Yard where real detective work gets done.

Chapter 6

Bowles's return to his office after meeting with Chief Inspector Carrie was nothing short of chaotic. Calls from the media, calls from the passengers of the *Queen's Speed*, calls from Crown Life Insurance, Ltd., and notes of a thousand other calls buried Bowles's desk. In typical Bowles style, he grabbed them all up in one great handful and threw them unceremoniously into the rubbish can. Then he picked up the phone to do some work.

His first call was to British Radio and Wireless. He asked for all records pertaining to ship-to-shore communications on the evening preceding the death of Millicent Prestwood.

His second call was to the social editor of the *London Times*. He requested copies of all articles, pictures, etcetera, which had run of Millicent Prestwood in the last three months. He asked for and scheduled a lunch on Wednesday with the social editor herself, one Myra Leighton-Thorpe. He then phoned Captain Harvey Clark and asked for yet another chat, possibly later that day. Finally, he called Jeffrey Hargreaves, the investigator for Scotland Yard who was scouting Charles Collett's drug-related activities for Chief Inspector Carrie.

After trading phone messages with Hargreaves, Bowles finally spoke to him after 5:00 P.M., on Monday. Bowles needed answers, and Hargreaves was as good a place as any to start.

"Investigator Hargreaves, Inspector Parkington Bowles here. I have been assigned to the matter of Millicent Prestwood's death. I understand that you have been studying certain drug-related crimes of late involving one Charles Collett and that you might have come across something which could help us get to the bottom of Mrs. Prestwood's death," Bowles explained.

"Chief Inspector Carrie informed me that you might call. How may I be of help to you?" the young investigator asked in a tired voice.

"Mr. Hargreaves, while following Mr. Collett, did you observe him often in the company of Bethany Ann Prestwood?"

Hargreaves responded, "Yes, I often followed Charles Collett and found him to spend a great deal of time with Miss Prestwood. As I understand it, they are to be married soon."

"Yes . . . yes they are, Mr. Hargreaves. Now, I know that this is a wild shot, but did you notice any changes in their relationship or in the patterns of their time together in the week before Mrs. Prestwood's death? Did they keep the same routines? Did they seem to get along the same? Did they seem to smile as much? Did they seem to be having fun together?" Bowles carried on, knowing that he was grasping for straws. He hoped that if Collett had been contemplating murder, his conscience might have given him trouble .

"Not really, Inspector," Hargreaves said pensively. "Collett always seemed to be having a good time."

"Did you take photographs of them together?" Bowles asked routinely.

"Of course, Inspector. We shot dozens of rolls of film of them over the last few weeks. You are welcome to view them at my office at your leisure," the young man said helpfully.

"Please have them all sent at once to my office. I will view them here and have them returned to you when I have completed my review," Bowles said, reasserting his seniority and ego.

Realizing that it was not worth the fight, Bowles's youthful colleague assured him. "Certainly, Inspector Bowles. I'll have them to you first thing in the morning." Then he hung up without saying another word.

No sooner had Bowles hung up than he rang up the half-wit chef, Gerald Blume.

"Mr. Blume. This is Inspector Parkington Bowles. Yes, we met on the *Queen's Speed* after Mrs. Prestwood died. I was hoping that we might have dinner tonight. I would like very much to ask you a few questions," Bowles calmly requested.

Blume responded, "Inspector, it would be a great pleasure to take a meal with you this evening; however, I have already begun preparing my dinner. You are certainly welcome to join me, if you fancy roast duckling."

Bowles hesitated and then figured that chefs must eat like the rest of God's children—only better. So he gratefully accepted.

At 7:45, Bowles arrived at the lovely cottage of Gerald Blume, a gingerbread-looking thing, with blue trim accenting a massive dose of off-white paint. He was greeted by a hulking man with hands the size of hams and a head that Bowles figured had to be at least seventy centimeters around. Strangely, his handshake was so soft that it wouldn't break an egg, and his voice was low and calm.

"Good evening, Inspector. I am so happy that you could come by tonight. Please come in and sit down." And with that Blume escorted Bowles to an easy chair where they began a conversation, the direction of which Bowles could not plan.

"Mr. Blume."

"Gerald, please, Inspector. Gerald will do nicely."

"Okay. Then Gerald it shall be! Tell me, Gerald, was there anything unusual about dinner the night before Mrs. Prestwood's death? Like, was there any arguing? Was the conversation angry? Or anything else of the sort?"

"Oh, no, Inspector. Everything at dinner was great. The veal was well received and the people seemed to be having a real fine dinner. That always makes me proud. No, they ate their dinner, had dessert, and then Dr. Steed proposed a toast to the chef. When he did that I got real nervous, because I hadn't set out any after-dinner liqueurs. But he didn't seem to mind. He just pulled out his flask, poured a bit of the contents into everyone's coffee, proposed the toast, and they all drank up."

"Did you spend any time with Mrs. Prestwood after dinner on the night before her death?" Bowles said, digging in at once.

"No, sir, Inspector. After dinner I remained in the galley as I always do. I cleaned up the dishes and stowed all of the pots, pans, and things I had out to make dinner. I was about to finish my work when I heard an awful row coming from one of the cabins. I hurried out to make sure that everything was all right. When I got to the top deck, I heard that it was Mrs. Prestwood and Mr. Collett shouting at each other. I don't like shouting; I get scared when people shout," Blume explained as he dropped his eyes from the inspector's gaze.

"Were you scared that night, Gerald?" the inspector asked carefully.

Blume, keeping his eyes lowered, answered quietly, "Yes, I was. It always scares me when Mrs. P. gets upset. When Mr. P. was alive, he took real good care of his wife. But after he was gone, she had to take care of herself, and I don't know if she was any good at it. So, anyway, I went back to the galley and worked harder than ever to keep busy and stay away from the arguing."

"So after that you didn't see Mrs. Prestwood alive again; is that right, Gerald?" Bowles continued.

"That's right."

"Gerald, what did you do the rest of the night?"

"Well, Inspector, I went to my cabin at about 8:30 and tied flies. It's my hobby, you know."

Bowles thought how improbable it was that a man of the size and strength of Gerald Blume would find his enjoyment in cooking and tying fishing flies. Each activity required a delicate touch, hardly imaginable considering the massive fingers and hands of this gentle giant.

"Of course, Gerald. Did you speak to anyone else that night?"

Blume thought carefully and then remembered, "Yes, sir, I did. At about 10:30, I received a call from Captain Clark. He asked me to make Mrs. Prestwood a cup of herb tea to help her calm her upset stomach and allow her to rest."

"Did Mrs. Prestwood often ask for tea late at night, Gerald?" Bowles pressed in gently.

With a huge smile, Blume answered as if remembering a happier time. "Yes, sir. Mrs. P. often called for tea at night. She always told me that I made the finest tea in Great Britain. She was a nice lady," Blume said, the smile disappearing from his face.

"But Gerald, you told me a moment ago that you did not see Mrs. Prestwood again that night. Did you forget the tea?"

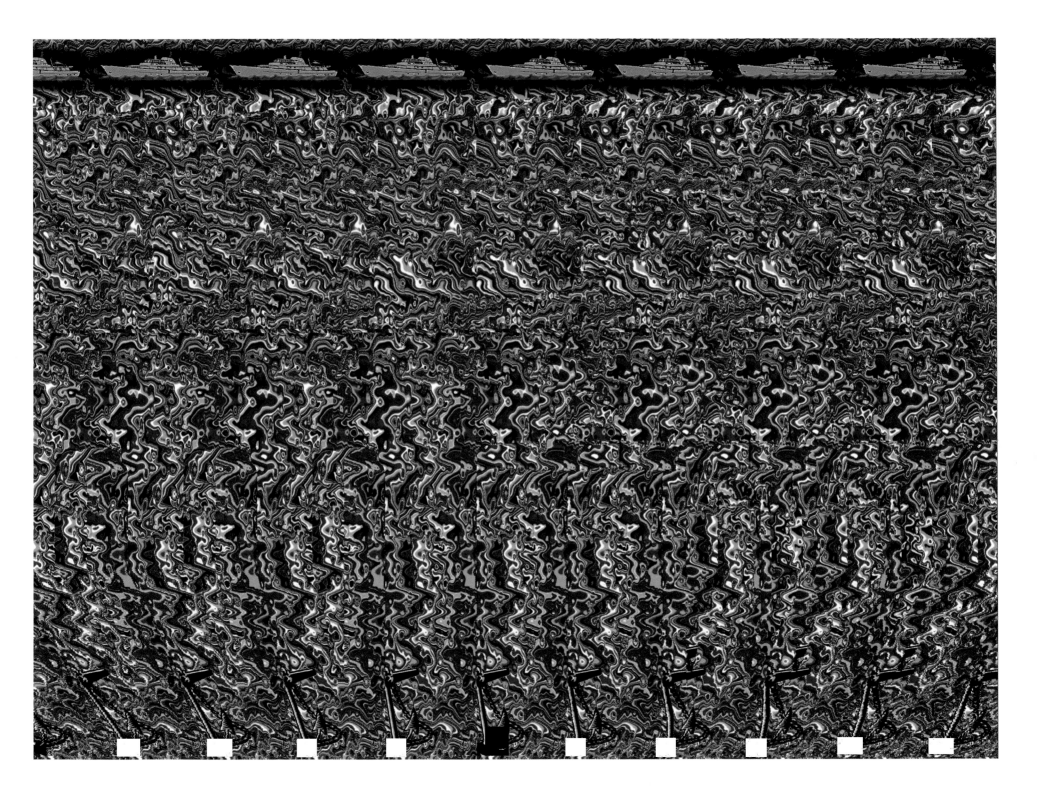

"I don't think I saw her again, Inspector. Let me think. I went to the galley. Made the tea. Was cleaning up . . . that's it! I didn't see Mrs. P., because as I was leaving the galley with the tea, Bethany was coming down for a snack. You know, she's a nice lady. She's just like her father. She always is nice to me. And she is sure pretty, too," rambled the grown man, carrying on like a ten-year-old.

"Gerald, please tell me what happened after you saw Miss Prestwood," Bowles asked, his anticipation rising.

"She asked me what I was doing, and I told her that I was taking a pot of tea to her mother. She sat in the galley and talked to me for a couple of minutes until I told her that I had to go before the tea was spoiled. Mrs. Prestwood only likes her tea to be steeped for about five minutes. She thinks it's bitter after that. Anyway, she told me that she would take it to her mother since she was going to see her anyway. I told her that her mother might not like me not doing my job, but she told me that she would take care of everything. So she took the tea to her mother and I went back and went to bed," Blume explained innocently.

Bowles knew that he had gotten about as much as he was going to get from this simple soul; however, he felt compelled to go further. "Gerald, did Bethany behave normally the night you gave her the tea?"

"Oh, Inspector, I don't know. She's always nice, and she was certainly nice that night, too. Maybe she did talk more than she usually does. She just hung around and talked to me real nice. She was real calm, and I like that a lot. When she left, she even gave me a hug. She's real nice like that."

Sensing that it was time to drop the questioning for now, Bowles closed his notepad and made ready for the feast promised by Blume. As he enjoyed the meal and the chat with its creator, however, he could not escape the feeling that things were beginning to make sense. He supposed that it would have been easy enough for Bethany to have slipped something into her mother's tea. But why on earth would she? It just didn't make sense. But then, the world was making less and less sense to Park Bowles anyway.

As they finished dinner, Bowles attempted one more volley of

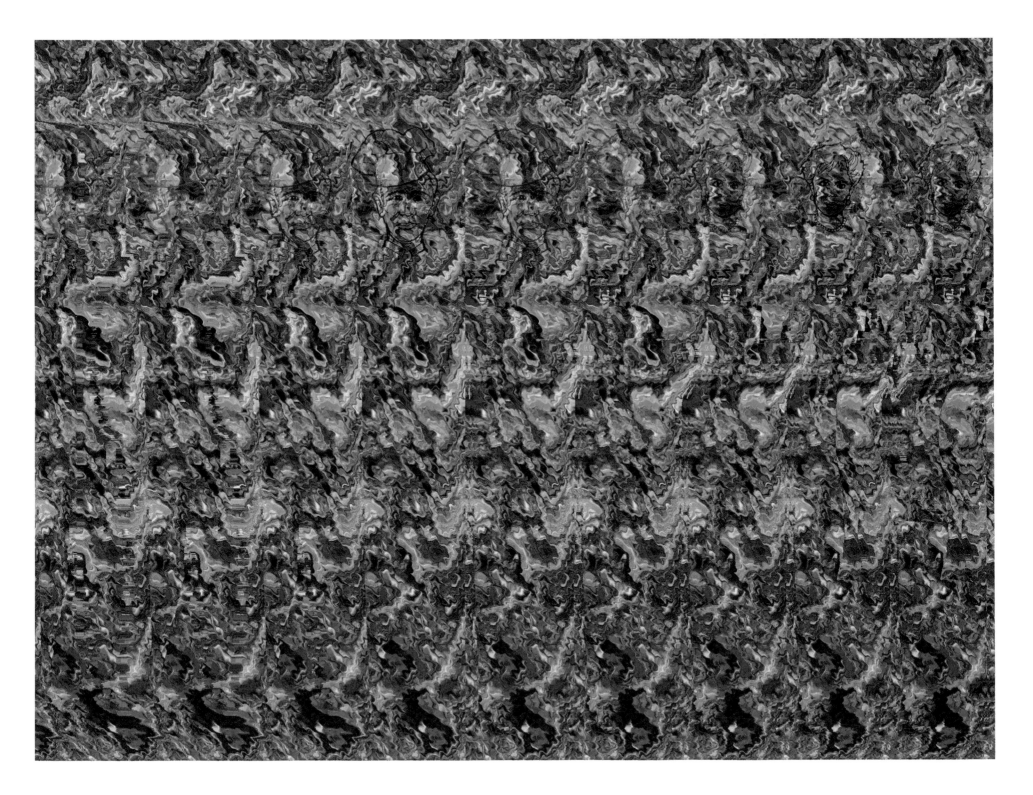

questions to his good-hearted host. "Gerald, did you prepare meals for the Prestwood family both at home and on the ship?"

"Oh, Inspector, I did all of the cooking at the Prestwood home. That's how it's been for years."

"Was Captain Clark a regular dinner guest?" Bowles asked.

Thinking a bit, Blume responded, "Lately he has been by more than he used to be. But since Mr. Prestwood died, it's been Dr. Steed who is around a great deal. He comes and goes almost every day, and he's often in and out several times a day."

"And of course, Mr. Collett is a frequent visitor," Bowles added.

"Not really all that much. I think that he often travels, so he comes to dinner maybe once a week," the chef said as he picked up the dishes and fled to the kitchen.

Following his lead, Bowles scooped up a handful himself and stacked them clumsily beside the stainless-steel sink where Blume silently rinsed the remaining scraps. "You don't care much for Mr. Collet, do you Gerald?"

Shifting his eyes to hide his guilt, he answered, "He scares me Inspector. I don't think I trust him."

Shortly thereafter, a stuffed inspector from Scotland Yard waddled down the steps from Blume's cottage and returned home, where he topped off the perfect repast with a cognac.

As he lay in his bed thinking about his pleasant conversation with the kindly giant, Bowles felt the unease that he knew well. The picture was becoming clearer, but still he couldn't make out the detail. Maybe tomorrow.

———❦———

Carefully, she freed herself from his arms and slipped from between the rustling silk sheets. Without a sound, she lowered herself from the raised four poster and touched the cold floor with ghostly lightness to avoid the creaking of the century-old maple. Momentarily, she saw herself as a wraith floating across the floor and down the thickly carpeted stairs in the dead of night as she proceeded resolutely to the first-floor study. There from the heavy oak cabinet, she withdrew the one thing that could assure her wealth and happiness and the elimination of her fears.

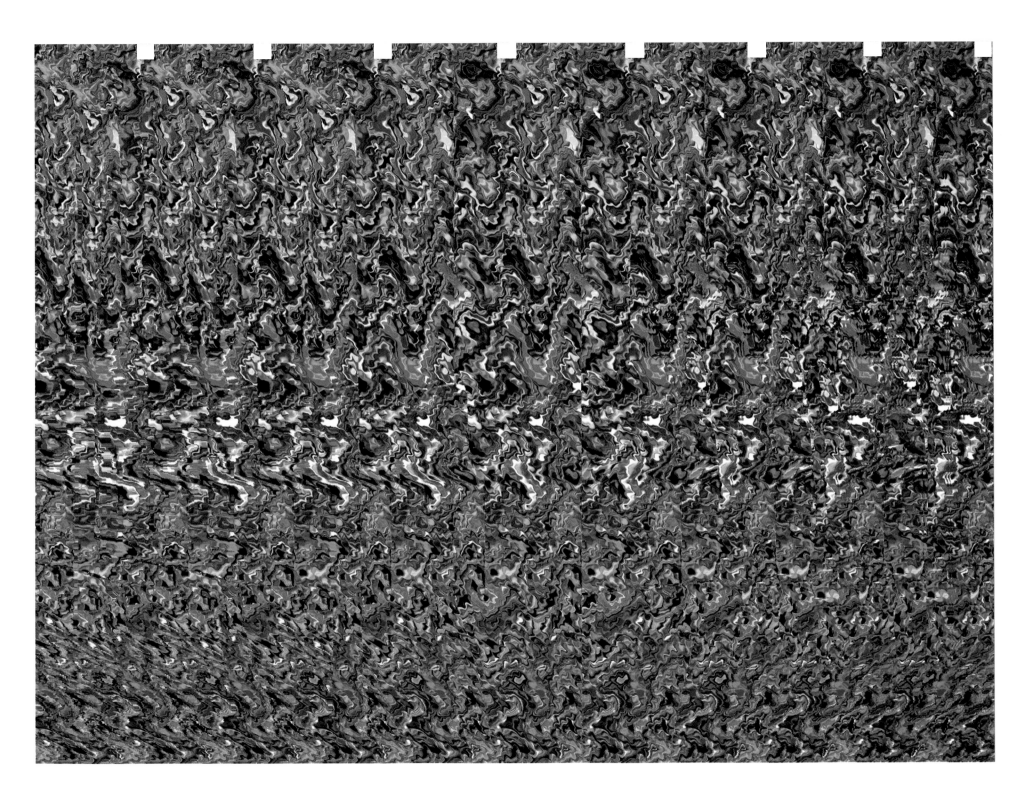

Carefully wrapping it in a cloth, she placed it in her bag and silently left the home at 3232 Abshire Common.

Chapter 7

The morning seemed unusually beautiful as H. Parkington Bowles stepped out of his door on Tuesday, July 31. The night of good investigative work coupled with little drink and excellent fare made him ready to tackle the death of Millicent Prestwood with renewed vigor.

His first call of the morning was to invite Charles Collett to come by his office. Collett agreed to stop by while out running errands about the city that morning. When he arrived at Scotland Yard, it was obvious that he was a great deal less taken with the morning's beauty than was Bowles.

"What now, Inspector?" groused the impatient young man.

"Mr. Collett, I was hoping that you could answer a couple more questions for me." Without waiting for permission, Bowles forged on. "On the night before Mrs. Prestwood died, I understand that you had words with her. Is that correct?"

Collett relaxed a bit and shifted slightly in his chair as if to signal that he was about to share a well-kept secret. "Inspector, I know that you have spoken to many of the others and I'm certain that you are a bright man. Let's not waste each other's time. Yes, we had a fight, and no, that was not really all that uncommon."

"Did you see Bethany later that night, Charles?" Bowles asked, trying to make the most of the young man's newfound cordiality.

"Inspector, on a ship like the *Queen's Speed*, we see each other quite frequently," Collett responded in a condescending tone, signaling the end of their *détente*.

Bowles stiffened and clarified, "Of course, but did the two of you spend time together after your argument?"

"Yes, we did. Bethany called me on the intercom and asked me to meet her in the galley for a snack at 10:30. As I approached, she was leaving and I walked with her to her mother's cabin, where we spoke for a moment or two until I headed topside to take over for Captain Clark. There he informed me of our course change to return to London and left. I remained at the bridge

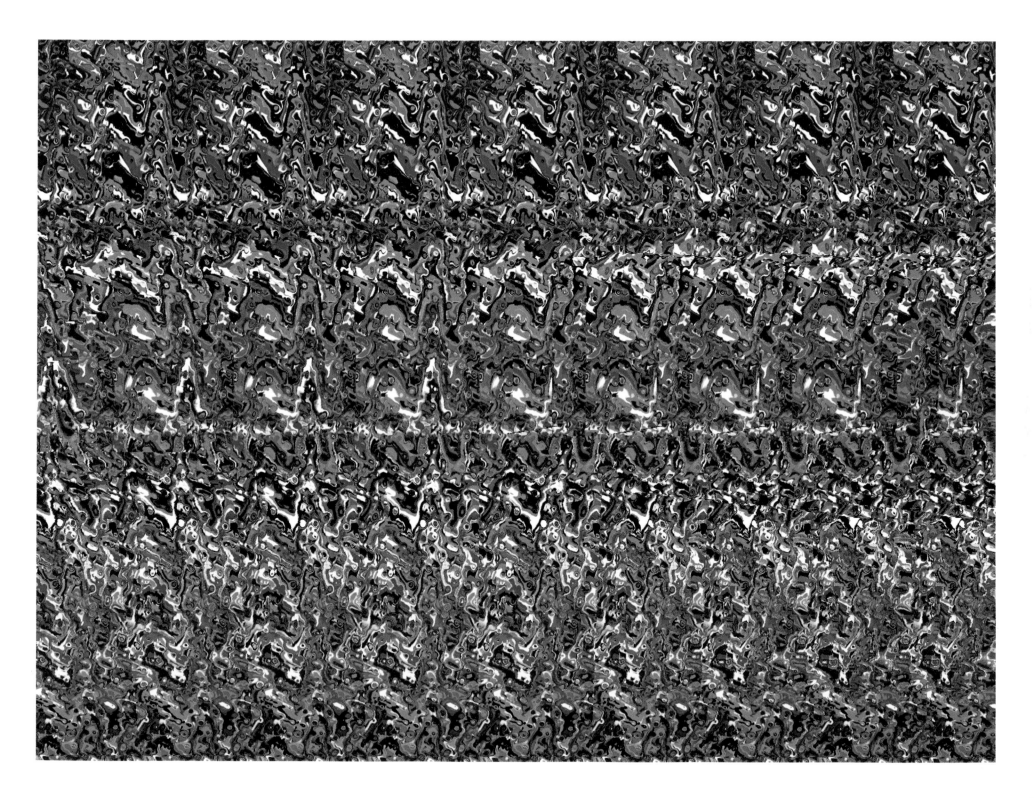

until about 6:30 A.M., when Clark took over for me. From there, I went directly to my cabin, where I was awakened at about 7:30 with the news of Mrs. Prestwood's death. I immediately changed my clothes and went topside, and stayed there until we reached London."

"You're beginning to sound as though you're searching for a murderer, Inspector?" asked a much more serious Collett.

"Did you kill her, Charles?" Bowles asked simply.

"Inspector, there is no secret that we did not get along well. And there is nothing I want in this world so much as to marry Bethany. But I would not kill to do so. Even if Millicent cut Bethany out of the will and distanced her-self from us, it wouldn't matter. We are in love, whether Millicent is alive or dead. Whether we have money or not. No, Inspector, I did not kill Millicent Prestwood, but neither do I grieve her. She was a mean and hateful woman, and I really don't give a whit that she has passed on, naturally or otherwise."

"Assuming that she didn't die of natural causes, who could have done such a thing?" Bowles asked matter-of-factly.

"If she was killed and I had to pick a murderer, I'd put my money on Clark," Collett said as he pulled his left hand out of his pocket, unwrapped a peppermint, and tossed it into his mouth. "As you undoubtedly are aware, I run with a pretty tough crowd. Well, I know that Harvey Clark owes money to people all over Europe. He's a compul-sive gambler, and a bad one at that. There are those who would have broken every bone in his body by now, except that they thought that he'd eventually get the money he needs to pay them back from Millicent. Maybe he couldn't wait and had to take matters into his own hands. I don't know how he planned to get it, but I know his time was running out."

Bowles responded, "Did Millicent know of his gambling?"

"I am certain that she did. He and Mr. Prestwood often ran off together and lost thousands. But after Mr. Prestwood passed, Clark couldn't reign in his habit," Collett explained.

"What about your fiancée, did she hate her mother enough to kill her?" Bowles probed.

"Beth is wild, but not that wild. She could not kill—not even

someone so hateful as Millicent. She is going to be my wife. I know her better than anyone, and I know that she just couldn't do such a thing," Collett stated with such resolve that Bowles truly believed that he meant it.

With that, Bowles bade Collett good-bye and leaned back until the back of his cane rocker dented the wall behind his Spartan desk. Absentmindedly, he picked up the envelope of pictures which he had received from the young Scotland Yard investigator Hargreaves and started leafing through them as his brain drifted off on a thousand other issues.

As he viewed the surveillance shots of Collett, he was struck by the number of shots that were taken of Collett leaving the home of Bethany Prestwood. Each picture was captioned with a time and date stamp in the lower right corner, imprinted automatically by the camera. It struck him that the investigators must have often camped out at Bethany's home to pick up the trail of Collett from the first of the day. As he fought with his anger over the poor quality of detective work that resulted in such a sloppy practice, he was dumbstruck by a photo dated June 27 at 7:20 A.M.

Photo number 627-46 showed not Collett, but a much older and heavier man leaving the premises on that summer morning. Unfortunately, Bowles was unable to determine the identity of the man. Immediately, he phoned Allen Caldwell, the head of the crime lab which was housed in an adjoining building.

"Allen, my friend. This is Park Bowles. How've you been? Long time no see."

"What you mean is, Park, is that it's been a long time since you've needed a favor," the technician retorted without a hint of warmth.

Bowles was undaunted. "Well, Allen, it's always a pleasure to talk with you, too. But since you are obviously not one to let bygones be bygones, let me tell you what I need. You don't have to be my mate to do your job, do you?"

"What is it, Bowles?"

"I have a photo taken by one of our surveillance teams and I need some photo enhancement done on it. I believe it might be of great help in getting to the bottom of the Prestwood matter," Bowles explained.

"The same Park Bowles. You think that all we do is wait around

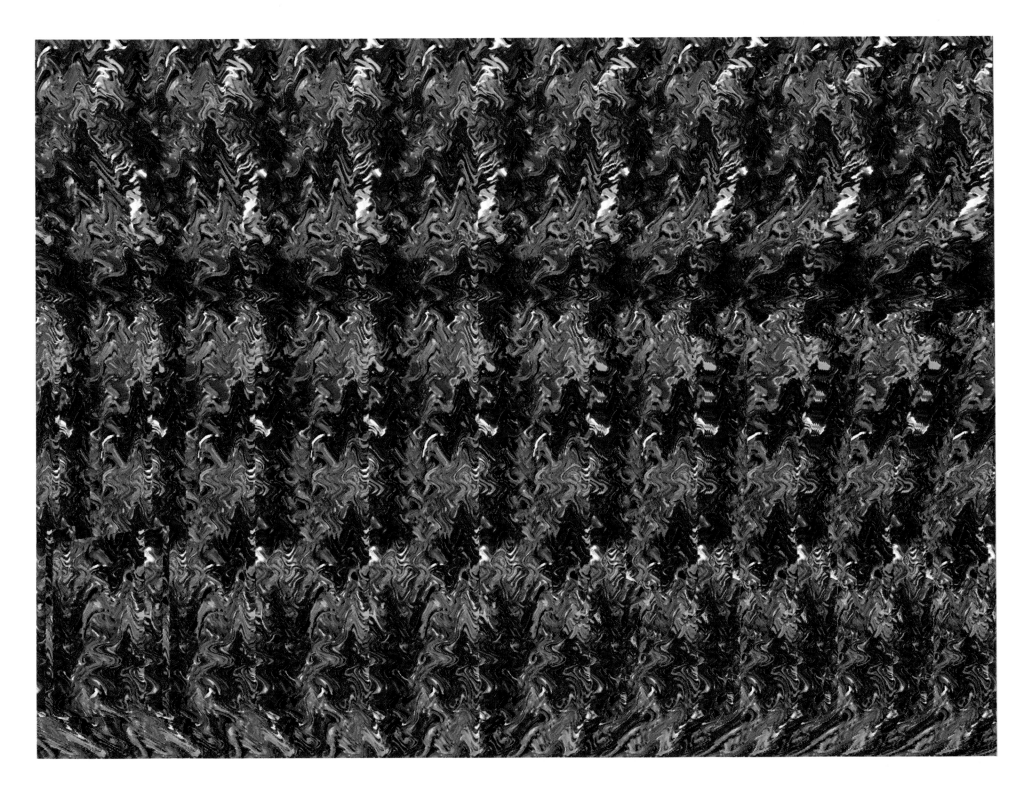

for your call for help. And then you speak about 'The Prestwood Case' as if I gave a care. Nevertheless, if you'll dirty your shoes by stepping into our side of the street, I'll get to it when I can," Caldwell hissed.

"Stick it in your ear, Caldwell!" Bowles shouted, slamming down the phone. He needed answers *now*, and the bureaucrats were playing turf games. He'd get it done himself rather than kiss their backsides.

Tired, Bowles slumped down into his chair and reflected on the exchange with Caldwell and considered, just for a moment, his failure to be elevated to chief inspector. Then he gathered himself and resolved to find a private photo shop where they could help him identify the man in the picture—without a lecture.

It was 9:00 P.M. before Bowles returned home from finding a German man named Karl Keisel, who had promised that by the next night Bowles would be able to tell the brand of watch the man in the picture wore, not to mention his identity. This victory was a small one for Bowles as he realized that he was fighting not only the criminals, but also his colleagues.

Lying in bed, Bowles unconsciously picked up the phone and dialed up Maggy Downes-Farrington. The sound of her voice shook him to consciousness and he stumbled all over himself as he tried to think up a good excuse for his call.

"Park, you sound awful," she announced. "Have you been back on the bottle?"

"No, Maggy, but I might as well be. I've lost my edge and I'm not making the progress on the Prestwood case I should be," he said, his self-pity almost dripping through the phone line.

"Let me give you some of your own advice, Park. Get off your backside and do your job. The Park Bowles I know wouldn't be wallowing in self-pity. Right now he'd be focused on stopping a murderer," she said with more compassion than it came out. "Now, good night. I'll talk to you in the morning."

Chapter 8

The next morning did indeed bring to Park Bowles a renewed vigor for his work. Just having someone like Maggy care

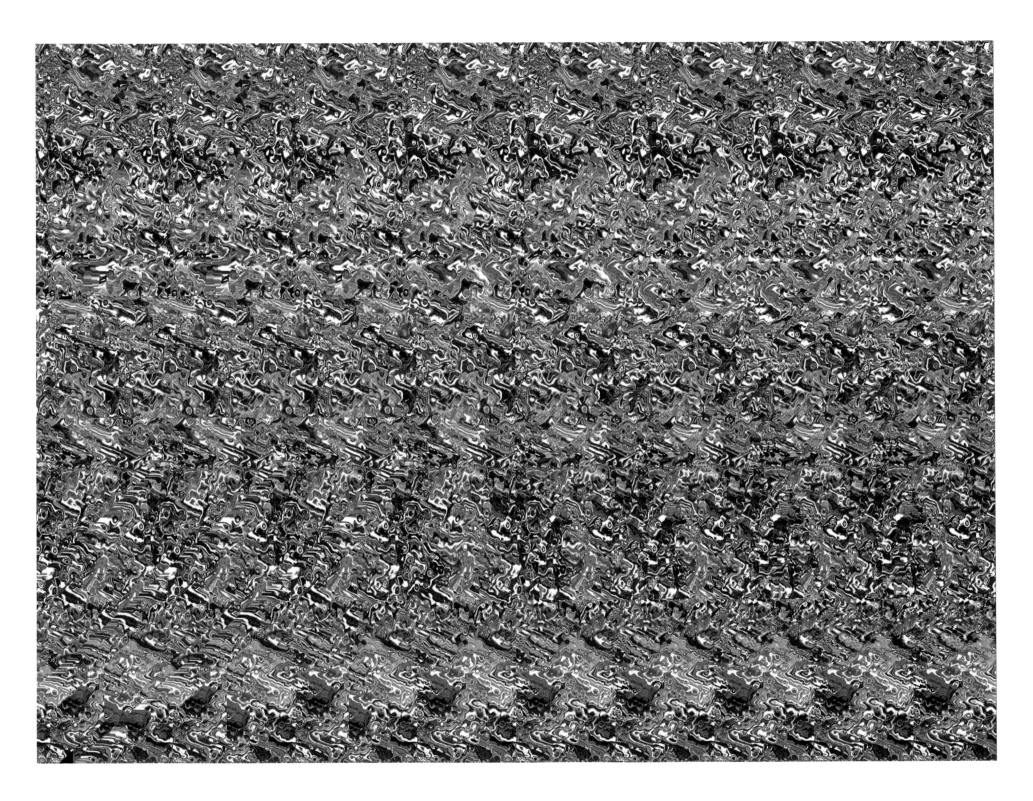

enough to kick him in the pants felt good, and he slept well with the thought of her steadily in his mind.

Also firmly in his mind was his belief that the time had come for him to have a long talk with Bethany Ann Prestwood. He had wanted to hold off meeting with her until he had learned what he could from the others. After all, she had the very best motive and all the opportunity in the world. In his newfound sense of mission, he simply forgot that rich, young women don't get up by 6:30 A.M., which explained at once why her response was ice-cold when he awoke her with his call. Irrespective of his thoughtlessness, however, she agreed reluctantly to come by his office before lunch for a short interview. While she clearly was not enamored with the idea of speaking with Bowles, she knew it was inevitable and so decided to get on with it.

When Bethany arrived, Bowles couldn't help recall the grossly sexist remark of his assistant, Colf. Sexist? Maybe. Accurate? Absolutely. She was a real looker, which made interviewing her a two-edged sword: Her beauty could make a man lose his train of thought; however, it also gave him very little reason to hurry through the interview.

"Thank you for coming down, Miss Prestwood. I'm certain that the last few days have been difficult for you, and I'm afraid I must deliver even more bad news: Your mother was killed," he said, his eyes glued on hers as he searched for any telltale sign. "She was poisoned."

At once she broke down in tears, burying her face deep within her hands until after twenty or thirty seconds, she slowly straightened and drew a deep breath.

With the look of a cornered animal and a voice as cold as steel, Bethany Ann Prestwood slowly and precisely stated, "Clark. He's your man. I have no proof, but he's been up to something. For the last couple of months he's been closing in on my mother. He's a loser and she couldn't see it. I told her he was bad news. And when he hit her up for 250,000 pounds last week that proved it. But she wouldn't believe me. She defended him while condemning me for wanting to be with Charles. Her wickedness and stubbornness have come back to haunt her."

"Why did Clark want to borrow so much money?"

"He told her that he was beginning a charter service for those days when she did not require his services. But that was a lie, and I told her so. He's so deep into the bookmakers that he could never crawl out without her help. All I got from my mother by trying to be honest was her spite. She said I was so bitter about my father that I didn't want her to be happy with any other man."

"So, your mother didn't give him the loot?" Bowles asked.

"She wanted to, but I talked her into waiting before she did anything. The man's rotten, but she wouldn't see it," the young woman said, shaking her head slowly.

"I keep hearing that you had the best reason to kill her. You hated her, you stand to inherit a fortune, and you certainly had plenty of opportunity," Bowles challenged.

"There are those who have the heart to kill and those who don't. No, Inspector, I couldn't kill anyone, even someone as mean and hateful as my mother," she confided.

"Why did you decide to take your mother's tea to her on the night before she died? You don't usually do that, do you?"

"Who told you that?" she demanded.

"Beth, it's irrelevant how I became aware that you took her the tea. What *is* relevant is why on that particular night you felt compelled to serve her personally," Bowles asked, his antennae telling him that he was closing in on a raw nerve.

"Inspector," she began, "I spent a couple of hard hours in my cabin alone thinking about the argument mother had with Charles on the night before she died. I had decided that it was time for me to grow up and stand for what I believed. I believe in Charles, and I want to marry him. I couldn't face any longer the criticism and embarrassment of being treated like a helpless child, so I decided to inform my mother of my decision to move away from London and from her.

"After reaching this decision, I resolved that the only way I would carry through with it was if I did it at that very moment. I called Charles on the intercom and asked him to meet me in the galley. I wanted to tell him what I was about to do."

"Why the galley?"

"I had been crying and my throat was dry. I planned to take a drink to Mother's room with me, and the cold beverages were kept in the galley. When I arrived there, I ran into Gerald Blume, who was preparing Mother a bit of tea. While I waited for Charles, Gerald and I had a lovely talk until I needed to go to Mother's cabin, with or without talking to Charles.

"No sooner had I stepped from the galley than I met Charles. I explained to him what I was about to do. He told me that he would support anything I wanted, and so I left for Mother's cabin."

Bowles asked, "At what time did you arrive at her cabin?"

"Probably about 10:45."

"What happened then?"

"Mother answered the door and was still very upset. I gave her the tea and began to talk with her about Daddy, Charles, and a whole range of things. I honestly think that she was trying to understand me, but too much had happened between us. I told her of my plan to leave and she was shattered. She told me that I was all that she had left and didn't know how she could carry on. That was one of the few times she has ever opened up to me at all. It was very emotional and, in the end, we agreed that I had to live my own life. When I left, I felt closer to her than I had in months. At least I have that consolation."

As Bethany Ann Prestwood finished her story, Bowles looked her in the eye, hoping that she was being honest with him. Personally, he wanted her to be the reconciled daughter, but professionally he had his doubts.

"Did you discuss your premature return to London?" Bowles asked, trying hard to keep his notes up with Bethany's soliloquy.

"Mother informed me that she had instructed Captain Clark to make a new heading for London with the purpose of changing her will to include a provision that would have cost me millions if I were to have married Charles. After our discussion, though, she said that we should keep the appointment with Trevor Moss. We cried a lot and shared a great deal of our hurt. In the end, she understood my need to have my own life. She told me that she would provide me with a lump sum which would free me to live my own life; however, that

would be the extent of my inheritance. The rest, except for a few small bequests, would be put into trusts for charity."

"Unfortunately, this plan was never put in place, Miss Prestwood. Is that correct?" Bowles asked, buying time while he thought through her story.

"That is correct, Inspector. But at least this way I can live in peace knowing that I had my mother's blessing in the end," she said, her voice, weighted down with emotion, trailing off.

"That certainly is of great value," Bowles said, nodding, although his mind could not resist the temptation to think that her mother's blessing was nice, but that tens of millions of pounds was no lump of coal.

"Tell me about how you left your mother that night," he continued.

"We parted close to midnight, with both of us emotionally drained."

"Did you and your mother share the tea?" he asked, both of them knowing what he was getting to.

She looked at Bowles with soft eyes and reassured him, "I am aware of what you're asking, Inspector. No, I did not drink the tea. As I said, I took a soft drink to my mother's room. And no, I didn't poison my mother. She had just given me a comfortable sum of money and her blessing. What more could I have wanted?"

That was the very question that stuck in Parkington Bowles's mind as he escorted Bethany Ann Prestwood to the lift at the end of the hall.

Before lunch, Bowles placed a call to Henry Colf and instructed him to go to the *Queen's Speed* and retrieve for analysis the teacup from Mrs. Prestwood's cabin, and all of the empty soda bottles on board, and take them to the chemical and fingerprint laboratories for analysis.

Next, he returned to his flat, where he reviewed the blueprint of the *Queen's Speed* to try to get a handle on the movements of the passengers on the night before Millicent's death. Finally, he called Maggy Downes-Farrington.

"Margaret, can you establish a time of death for Mrs. Prestwood?" Bowles asked seriously.

She responded with a laugh.

"Park, you only call me 'Margaret' in two instances—the

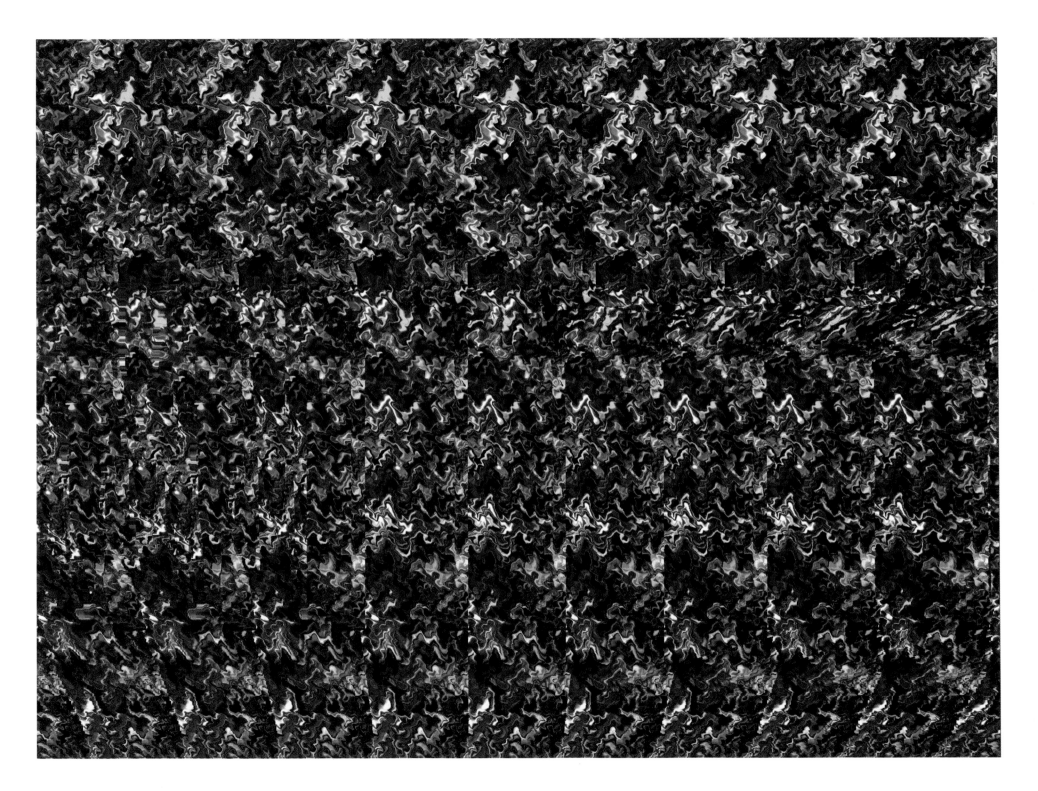

height of your passion or when you're closing in on your prey. I presume that this time it's because you're closing in."

"I may be, Maggy. It partially depends on what your report says."

She replied slowly as she leafed through the report, "Not much of value here, Park. It can only be established that she had been dead six to ten hours when the examiner first checked her at 10:00."

"This poison that was used, how long does it take to work?" he asked, hoping for a clear-cut answer.

"Sorry again, Park. It all depends on how much was used," she responded. "It could work quickly with a large dose or slowly with a smaller dose."

Bowles's hopes of a revelation seemed dashed by Maggy's report. On the other hand, that was the nature of the business, and Park Bowles had now picked up the scent. He knew instinctively that he was closing in, and that excited him.

Chapter 9

The approach of nightfall was irrelevant to Park Bowles. In his windowless, inner office, his thoughts retraced the details of Millicent Prestwood's last night of life. Mindlessly, he pored over the mountains of paperwork, which had begun to grow exponentially on his modest desk. He reread each line of his notes from his leather pad and reflected on the puzzle before him. As he was about to reread

the statements of the passengers for the dozenth time, he received a phone call.

"Inspector Bowles," came the voice, "this is Karl Keisel. I have completed the work on the photograph you asked me to work on, and it is ready for your inspection."

In his excitement, Bowles wanted Keisel to tell him to describe the man in the picture. But upon gathering his thoughts, he instructed the man to wait for him at his shop, a ten-minute drive which Bowles made in six.

Upon arriving at Keisel's shop, Bowles threw open the door and tore the photo from the frightened man's hand. At first glance, his body relaxed and a broad smile washed across his face as he once again smelled the blood of the kill.

Thursday morning arrived brightly as Park Bowles was filled with the energy that comes from adrenaline. He arrived at his office shortly after dawn and at once began to plan the day on a fresh page of his pad.

Until the hour became reasonable for outbound calls, he huddled with Colf and received a briefing on the lab reports. As he expected, the teacup seized from Millicent Prestwood's cabin showed no trace of anything but tea and cream. A similar review of the seized soda bottles proved that, indeed, Bethany Prestwood had handled several of them.

"Inspector, why are you not surprised that the teacup is clean?" the confused junior investigator asked. "I had expected that the poison was delivered with Mrs. Prestwood's tea. Why did you think otherwise?"

Bowles's lip curled slightly as he explained, "This crime was committed after a great deal of planning. Mrs. Prestwood taking tea was not an event that could be planned on; therefore, it could not have been the planned time for the delivery of the poison. Further, the poison, if administered in the correct dosage, would take hours to cause death, thereby eliminating the need for it to be administered immediately prior to the hoped-for time of death. Finally, Blume reported to me that when Captain Clark called down for tea for Mrs. Prestwood, he requested it (reading from his notepad) 'to help her calm her upset stomach and allow her to rest.' According to Margaret Downes-Farrington of the medical examiner's office, one of the reactions from ingesting chlorol nitrate on top of Drimatosin would be upset stomach and nausea."

"That's brilliant, Inspector. But if not administered with the tea, then when?" a chastened Colf asked.

"That is what we must determine next, my dear Mr. Colf," Bowles said with a relaxed smile.

With that, he asked Colf the status of the search for any trace of chlorol nitrate that had been used to commit the crime. Unfortunately, the lab reported that unless they got lucky it might take a while longer before the tests for the chemical were complete. Masking his frustration, Bowles asked his assistant to let him know at once when he had something.

The hour having arrived for proper citizens to be awake, 8:00 A.M., Bowles phoned Miles Carrie and asked what progress had been made with the young solicitor.

Carrie responded, "Young Mr. Moss has held his position firmly; however, his senior partner has called in a panic, offering to assist us in any way he could—short of breaking the law, of course."

"Of course. Ask him to look through the Prestwood assets and see if any of the other passengers held any ownership interest," Bowles instructed, enjoying greatly the feeling of being firmly in charge of the investigation. "Something Bethany said made me remember that a will isn't the only way to get money from rich folks."

After a breakfast of toast, jam, and Earl Grey, Park Bowles went di-rectly back to his office, where he carefully scrutinized the record of ship-to-shore communications on the night before the widow's death, hoping to find something that would tighten the noose around the neck of one of the suspects. Unfortunately, he found no record of calls, except for the one of which he was already aware between Clark and the solicitor, Trevor Moss. The only other listed con-nection was one of twelve seconds which he figured had to be an error. Dejected, he threw down his pad and slowly massaged his tem-ples until the price of the first call struck his eye.

In the right column was listed a price of seventeen pounds. Tracing the line back to the left, Bowles stared at the duration of the call: twenty-seven minutes. Flipping feverishly back through his notepad, he discovered the state-ment by Trevor Moss that "...the conversation had been brief." As he studied the call log, Bowles began to question how it was that a brief phone call took so long.

Dialing up Trevor Moss was a pleasure for Bowles.

"Mr. Moss, I shall move directly to the point. You have reported to me that your phone conversation on the night before Mrs. Prestwood's death was brief; howev-er, the phone company lists it as ex-tending past twenty-seven minutes. You have lied to me and I suggest you take this opportunity to come clean. Do so now and we let the past remain in the past. Refuse and I fry you and your career. How do you want to play it? You have ten sec-onds."

The line went silent as the young barrister fought with himself.

"What'll it be, Moss?"

"This is extortion."

"No, it's perjury and hindering an official investigation."

Five seconds passed, a blink to Bowles; an eternity to Moss, his mind blank with fear.

Faintly came, "Fine."

Several seconds more passed as the young man closed his eyes, wet with tears.

Then . . . "Yes, Inspector, Clark had somehow found out that Mrs. Prestwood had placed a tail on Collett. He then talked Mrs. Prestwood into allowing him to confront Collett on her behalf. I was instructed to tell Clark every-

thing that we had uncovered."

"So your time on the phone was spent telling Clark what your PI had found out on Collett?"

"That is correct."

"Is there anything else you would like to get off your chest, my boy?" goaded Bowles.

"Yes, there is," said the lawyer. "At shortly after midnight there was a fax transmission from Mrs. Prestwood, which I retrieved when I arrived at my office the next morning. It said only:

> Being of sound mind, I, Millicent Prestwood, hereby disinherit Bethany Ann Prestwood and leave her nothing under my will dated February 22, 1990.

"It was signed by Millicent Prestwood and dated in her hand."

"Is that amendment a legal codicil to her will, Mr. Moss?"

"Possibly, possibly not, Inspector," stated the young man, comforted to be back in his own arena.

"Have you informed anyone else of this communiqué?"

"No, Inspector. I am awaiting instructions from Scotland Yard."

"Good boy," Bowles said, calmly replacing the receiver, a huge smile spreading across his face as he did so.

———◆———

Bowles immediately followed up with a call to Charles Collett.

"Mr. Collett, when we last spoke, you expressed that Captain Harvey Clark was a desperate man.

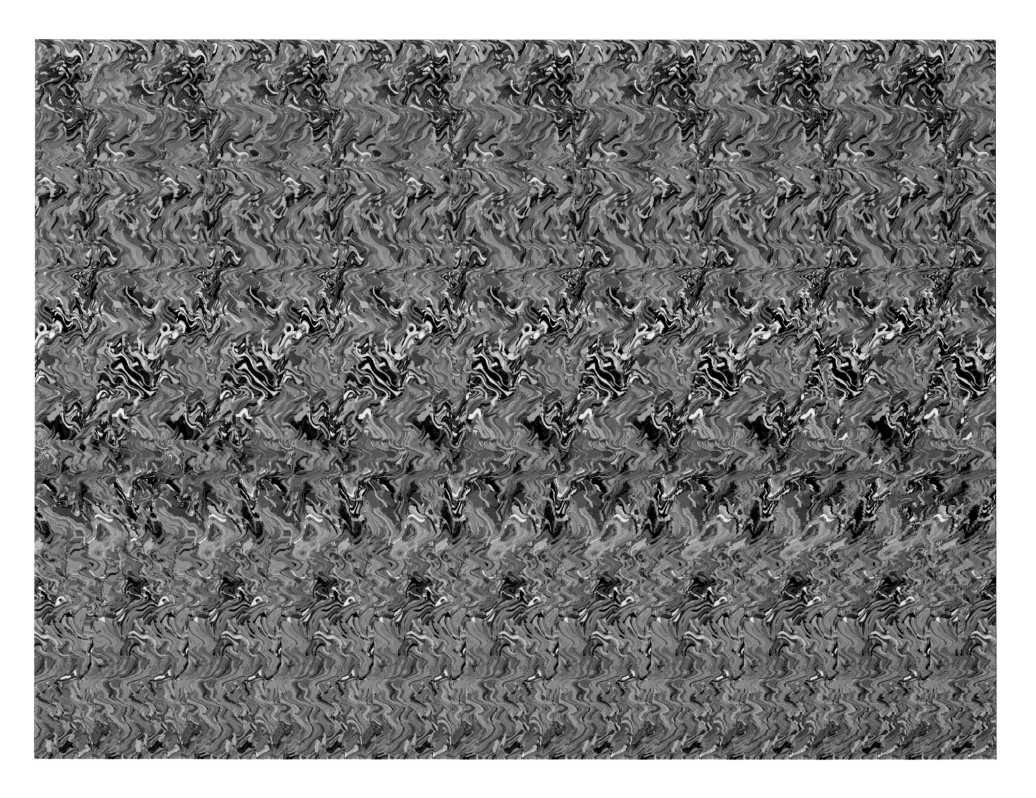

Did he ever approach you about money for his debts?"

After a brief silence, Collett responded, "Yes, Inspector, he did. I guess that you could call it an approach. When he came up to turn over the ship to me on the night before Millicent's death, he told me that he had all the proof he needed to bury my hopes of ever marrying Bethany. He told me that he had Millicent totally dependent on him and that if I would give him 250,000 pounds sterling, he would turn the story around and see to it that it never came to light."

"And what was your response?"

"I told him that he was a pathetic worm and that I didn't care what he told anybody. However, I did tell him that if he screwed around with me, I would make it clear to my friends that he never intended to, nor could he, pay the gambling debts he owed. I think he got the picture. After that, he gave me the new heading and went below."

"Mr. Collett, why didn't you tell me this when we talked the first time?" Bowles asked casually.

Shaking his head, Collett laughed. "Inspector, I can take care of myself. Losers like Clark are a dime a dozen, and since it didn't seem relevant to Millicent's death, I didn't mention it."

Bowles had dealt with many men like Collett and he understood exactly what Collett meant. He often thought that the nearest thing to an officer of the law was a crook, psychologically speaking. They both understood power and loved the game.

"Thank you, Mr. Collett," Bowles said as he replaced the receiver on the hook and sat back in his squeaky chair to contemplate the new information which was beginning to filter in.

———⊰•⊱———

Bowles's afternoon was cluttered with paperwork, updates for the Maritime Board, press conferences, and interviews. Everyone in Great Britain seemed interested in the death of Millicent Prestwood. Bowles thanked his lucky stars that he had concluded in time that there was something foul afoot. Had he not, the embarrassment would have been unbearable, not to mention the injustice.

Just after six, Bowles returned to his desk to find a stack of messages a couple of centimeters thick. Leafing through them he snatched out one from Colf that read: "re: chemical tests on *QS* passengers."

Bowles dialed Colf's mobile number from memory and waited impatiently for an answer. When Colf picked up, Bowles asked even before being greeted, "What'd they find?"

"Traces of the chemical that caused Mrs. Prestwood's death were found in the right front pocket of Collett's trousers . . . the ones he wore on the night she was poisoned. Things aren't looking so good for Mr. Collett, are they, Inspector?"

"Time will tell, Henry. Time will tell."

Chapter 10

By noon Bowles had wrapped up a series of secondary interviews with experts whose input proved conclusively how the murder had been committed, but did little to help him determine by whom. After bidding good-bye to the last one, Bowles received a call from Miles Carrie.

"Park, I just got off the phone with Trevor Moss's senior partner. As you might guess, many of the Prestwood assets were tied up in partnerships and other types of joint ownership. But only one would have involved a passenger on the *Queen's Speed*: Captain Harvey Clark."

"How so, Miles?" Bowles asked, his mind moving a kilometer a second.

"When Old Milton Prestwood bought the *Queen's Speed*, he placed the title in three names: his, his wife's, and Harvey Clark's," Carrie explained. "With both Mr. and Mrs. Prestwood out of the way, the ship belonged to Clark, as they say, 'lock, stock, and barrel.' It wouldn't pass through the will and there would be no waiting time after a death for him to take possession of the asset. Within a week he could have borrowed millions using it as collateral, and it wouldn't have even been public knowledge. Very clean. No insurance investigation, no probate of the will, nothing!"

"It was brilliant work, Park," glowed Carrie. "Do you think this is the key?"

"Time will tell, Miles. Time will tell."

Park Bowles had learned over the years that the only way to solve a complex problem was to put it in writing, where he could see and study it at his leisure. He pulled out a chalkboard he had used for over fifteen years and created a chart, each column of which was headed by the name of one passenger aboard the *Queen's Speed*. Over the next two hours he created a map of the case, which made clear all of the questions, but suggested few of the answers.

———◦———

Going through it all in his mind, Bowles still believed that any of the passengers could have done it; however, his focus was beginning to narrow.

It seemed clear to Bowles now that Captain Harvey Clark had a clear motive for killing Millicent Prestwood: quick cash. He certainly had the opportunity. But would Clark have had so much finesse? He'd go to her cabin, poison her drink, hope he didn't get caught. No, to Bowles, this was done with class. However, Clark's hidden motive and obvious opportunity seemed to strongly implicate him in the death.

Then there's Bethany. Based on the fax sent to Trevor Moss, it was now obvious to Bowles that either Bethany had lied to him about the reconciliation with her mother or that the old street fighter had feigned making peace with her daughter, only to financially disembowel her as soon as she left her room. Looking back through his notes from Clark's description of his attempted visit to Millicent's cabin on the night before her death, he realized that the sobs Clark heard could have just as easily been sobs of hatred and anger as they could have been sobs of reconciliation. With millions of pounds on the line and the beneficiary lying, Bethany was still a viable candidate.

As he mulled over that question, Bowles scanned the mountain of paperwork that obscured his desk and pulled from it the envelope labeled Karl Keisel Photography, Ltd. Slowly, as if drawing a fragile crystal from its sheath, he removed the dark, but clearly visible picture number 627-46 taken on June 27, at 7:20 A.M., of Dr. Jonas Steed stealing away from the home of Bethany Ann Prestwood. This piece just didn't fit, although decades of detective work had seasoned Bowles enough for him to realize that cases often are solved with the odd piece. Find out how the odd piece fits and

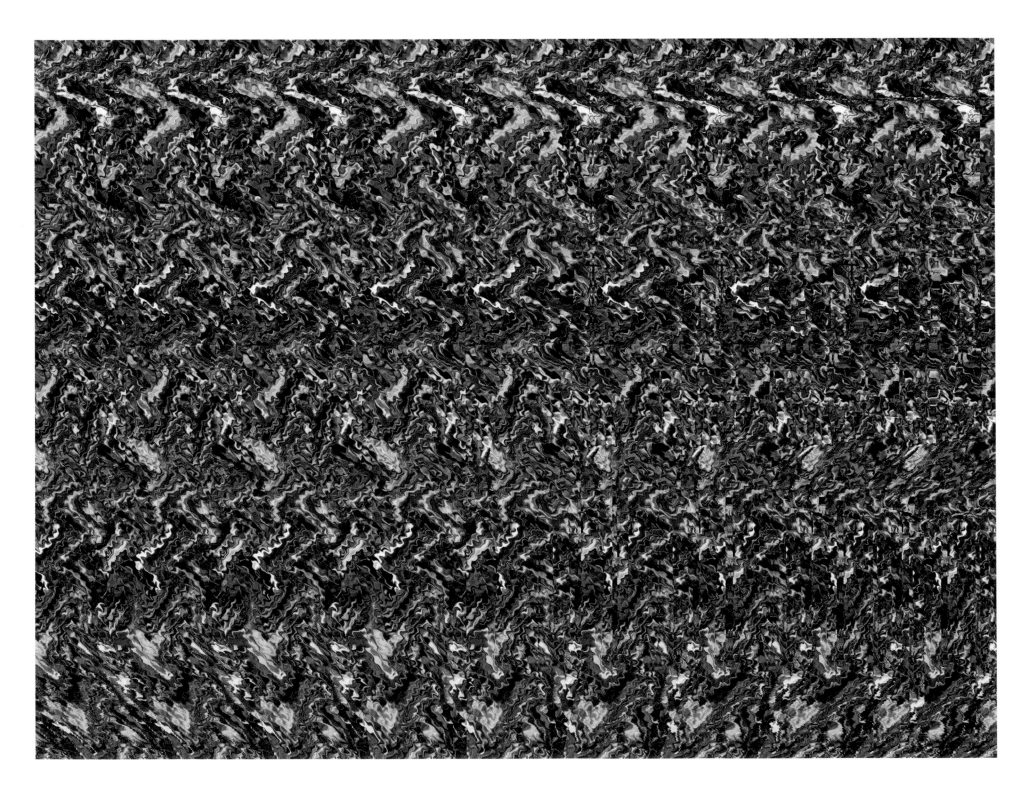

solve the crime. But still, why would this man, nearly three times Bethany's age, be sneaking out of her home before 8:00 A.M.? Drug treatment? Drug supply? Counseling? *Sex*?

Of course, Charles Collett was the prime suspect. Hatred, anger, passion, and greed all could have driven this man who was so familiar with the laws of the streets to expedite the removal of an obstacle. But why so careless as to leave evidence on the ship? Why do it himself? In his circles there are countless men who would have seen to her termination on his behalf. Quietly. Professionally. Accidentally.

About the only person that Bowles couldn't find a motive for was Gerald Blume. Once again,

though, in his experience Bowles had learned that the one who seems least likely is often the culprit. But surely not the half-wit Blume? Who knows?

With these thoughts gushing through his scrambled mind, Herbert Parkington Bowles did as he always did when his mind could go no farther in such situations: He reached for the bottle of Chivas which had solved (and created) countless problems for him over the years.

Chapter 11

Before dawn could awaken him, Park Bowles was staring at the blank ceiling above his bed as he mentally weeded through the volumes of information in which he knew was hidden the answer to Millicent Prestwood's death. Switching on the small lamp next to his bed, he pulled his leather pad from the jacket, which the night before he had thrown over the bedpost. He reviewed his notes carefully, especially those relating to Charles Collett and Harvey Clark.

Unwilling to sleep and unable to make progress, he decided to go to his office for another review of the information he kept there. Finishing a cup of strong coffee, he grabbed his key ring and headed for the door. As he stepped out, he nearly tripped over a small package wrapped in paper and tied with rough brown cord.

While stooping to lift it, his mind flashed with the picture of his wife nine years earlier, helplessly

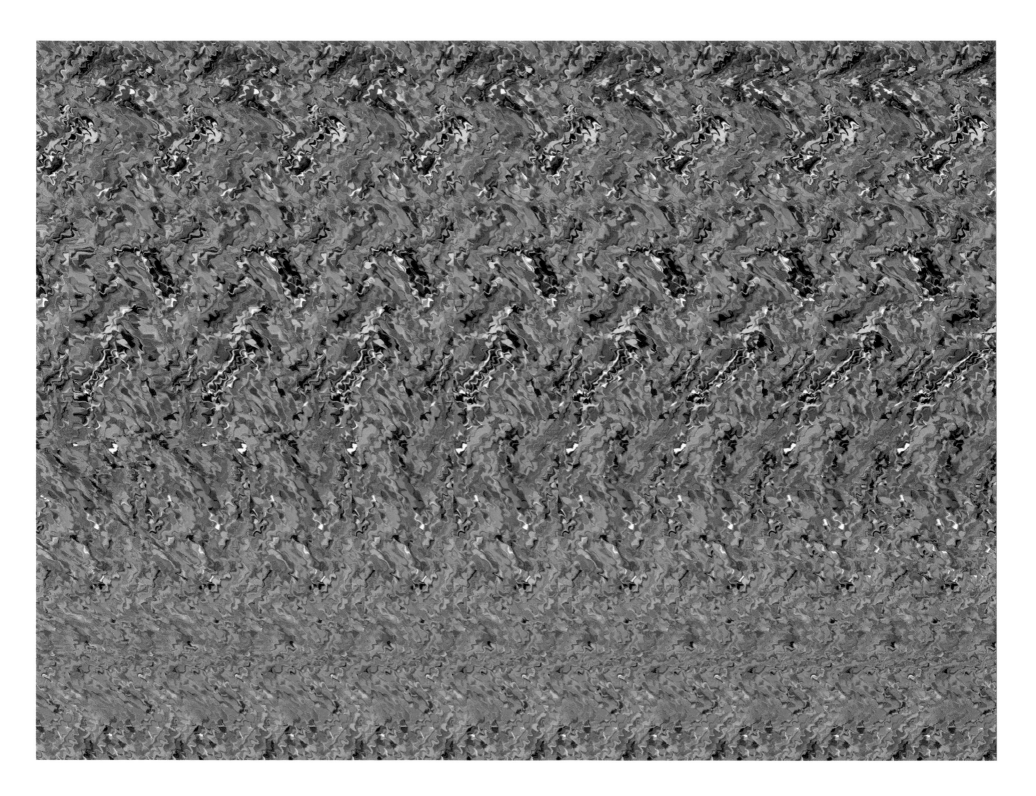

turning the key to the ignition a split second before his car exploded into fiery rubble. His hand slowly pulled back from the package and he stood there quietly remembering her. While life wasn't much without her, it was still life, and it was about all he had left. At that point he vowed to appreciate it a little more and hate it a little less.

He retreated back inside, where he placed a call that brought the bomb squad, a clearance of the building, and a visit from Miles Carrie.

After hours of commotion, it was determined that there was no bomb. Instead, the package contained a sterling silver flask wrapped in a soft cotton cloth. At once Bowles knew that he had seen it before, but was uncertain of where. Instinctively, he pulled from his pocket the little notebook and began to leaf through the pages. There at the very beginning, listed under the personal effects with which the passengers left the *Queen's Speed* and under the name of Dr. Jonas Steed, was "one liquor flask, silver." He stared at the flask for a moment and shook his head. Although he now understood, he nonetheless sent it along to the laboratory for analysis along with the following note:

Alan—

I know that I've been a bloody pain over the years and I wish that you would accept my apology.

HPB

P.S. Can you look this over for me and let me know what you find? I'd appreciate it.

The analysis, Bowles realized, was necessary only for proof. He knew that someone had delivered the flask anonymously to tip him off. But who was it that was setting Steed up? Did that person also put the poison in Collett's pocket? What of Clark's need for money and access to it through Millicent's death? What of Bethany's hatred and inheritance?

As the hours passed, Bowles sat quietly in front of his chalkboard and skipped between it and his leather pad. At midday, Alan Caldwell called to report that the flask carried the fingerprints of Dr. Jonas Steed and no one else. The flask also showed residue of chlorol nitrate, the chemical that had caused the death of Millicent Prestwood.

Bowles hung up the phone and stared at the photo of Steed exiting

Bethany Prestwood's home. As he did this, he mechanically dialed the number for Jonas Steed. He was surprised to have it answered by Steed himself after only the second ring.

"Dr. Steed. This is Inspector Parkington Bowles of Scotland Yard. There has been a development in the death of Millicent Prestwood that I would like to discuss with you. I would like to send a car for you in ten minutes so that we might discuss the issues."

Steed answered with decorum, but sounded far away. "Yes, Inspector. I understand. Please have the gentlemen come right over; I will be expecting them."

Bowles understood the air of resignation in Steed's voice and calmly placed a call to Miles Carrie.

"Miles, this is Park. Please have sworn out for me a warrant calling for the arrest of Dr. Jonas Steed for the murder of Mrs. Millicent Prestwood. He will be arriving at my office within the hour and I will serve him at that time."

Carrie had heard the tone in Park Bowles's voice before and he knew that Bowles had gotten his man. The details would wait . . . they always did. He also knew the anguish that Bowles felt when the betrayal of a friend threw one more handful of dirt on Park Bowles's view of humanity. Bowles drew no pleasure from his work, but at least some small measure of justice could now be served.

"Why, Park?"

Bowles's voice sounded weary and distant as he whispered, "Like always, Miles. Love and money." He hung up the receiver.

"Inspector Bowles, this is Colf. Steed is dead. I think that you should come here at once."

Maggy Farrington was always thrilled to hear from Park Bowles, even at this hour of the night, and she agreed at once to drive to his flat without so much as asking for a reason. She had heard the spectral voice before and she knew that she could not refuse. Upon her arrival, she was greeted by a softer version of the tough old bird that Park Bowles portrayed to others.

"Maggy, you've come to save me yet once more," he said, attempting without success to lighten the moment.

"Park, what is it?" she responded as she wrapped herself in the slack arms of the old man who peered at her through tired eyes.

Shaking his head as if he personally carried the weight of the world, he responded, "Maggy, I'm no longer able to keep all of this in perspective. Where did all of the hate come from?"

She remained silent and waited for him to continue to exorcise his pain.

"Millicent Prestwood was murdered with cold precision and planning by a man who had been one of her best friends for more than forty years. He had cared for her, delivered her child, and been accepted as family. He then took her daughter as his lover and together they plotted the death of an innocent woman. How can there be so much evil in the world?"

As Margaret Downes-Farrington moved closer to her distressed friend, she knew that she had no answers. "Park, tell me how you knew that Steed was the one."

Regaining strength from her presence he went on. "Collett really did love Bethany, and she loved him. Unfortunately, she wanted not only his love, but her mother's money. So she took matters into her own hands and preyed on the weakness of Jonas Steed to draw him to herself. She drove him to near madness with the kind of wild, nonsensical lust that an old man can only derive from a bright, young woman. She convinced him that Millicent would never abide the two of them together and that the only way their love could work was with Millicent gone. A crazy story, but one that thousands of old men gamble their lives and reputations on every week.

"Steed knew how to reduce to practically nil the odds of being found out. He fed Millicent the chlorol nitrate in her drink at dinner, when he proposed his toast and provided the liqueur from his flask. By knowing the dosage of Millicent's medication and the rough quantity of the chemical it would take to kill her slowly, he committed a nearly invisible crime. Had the chef, Blume, not relayed the story of the toast after dinner, I probably would never have determined the source of the poison."

Maggy interrupted, "And since chlorol nitrate is only lethal when combined with Drimatosin, no one else would have been affected by ingesting it."

"Precisely. And had that flask not have shown up mysteriously at my door, we would have had no proof to tie Steed to the crime in any event."

"So where did the flask come from? Or should I ask from whom did it come?"

"Bethany wanted some insurance to protect her backside. She figured that if the heat got too bad or if Steed's conscience got the better of him, she could always name him as the killer. Obviously, she took the flask back from Steed at some point and held it until it was needed."

"But the only trace of the chemical was on Collett. How did you figure that he wasn't involved?" Maggy asked, the conversation taking on a tone of urgency well beyond the current need.

"According to my notes, Steed left the *Queen's Speed* a full twelve minutes after the prior passenger. During this time, he apparently placed a trace of the poison in Collett's right front pocket, assuming that if the crime were detected all attention would be drawn to the man with the greatest motive. Unfortunately for the doctor, he failed to remember that Mr. Collett is left-handed. I was prepared to put the full press on Collett until I came across this tidbit, and I knew from that point on that Collett was being framed."

Maggy shook her head in wonder as she marveled at the man whose mind, while clouded by sadness and hatred, could keep a clear grasp of thousands of minute details. "Well, that explains Collett, but why didn't you focus on Clark after you found him holding the title to the *Queen's Speed* after her death?"

"Simply this. If Clark had known that Millicent had already been poisoned, why would he have tried to put the arm on Collett for money after he left Millicent's cabin. No, he's just lucky that he will now be able to pay off his debts . . . although with his luck at the track, he'll probably be back in the same soup again soon."

He continued, "I guess I never even considered the half-wit Blume. He loved Mrs. Prestwood and could never have turned against her. He just wasn't mentally capable of it. Unfortunately for Dr. Steed, however, Blume's memory isn't as weak as his logical functions. It was his recollection of the details of dinner that provided the solution to the case."

"Assuming that all of this conjecture is on the money, Park, how are you planning to tie all of this to Bethany? It's her word against yours, and there is no proof."

"Bethany's only miscalculation in an otherwise flawless plan was her failure to realize that Steed might one day come back to his senses. As he discovered the missing flask, he began to feel the circle tightening about him and realized that Bethany had betrayed him. Before he took his life, he posted to me this tape of the two of them discussing their plan. You see, he had insurance too; unfortunately, Bethany acted before he could use the tape to stop her."

"So she nearly got away with it. She would have inherited the money. Collett and she could marry free from Millicent's scourge and Steed would either take the coward's way out or rot in prison without proof of Bethany's complicity," Maggy said, shaking her head sadly.

"In the end, Maggy, Steed really did try to set the record straight. He wasn't the first old man to have his head and good sense turned by a pretty face," Bowles said as he closed the leather pad and tossed it onto the table beside him.

"Nor the last," whispered Maggy.

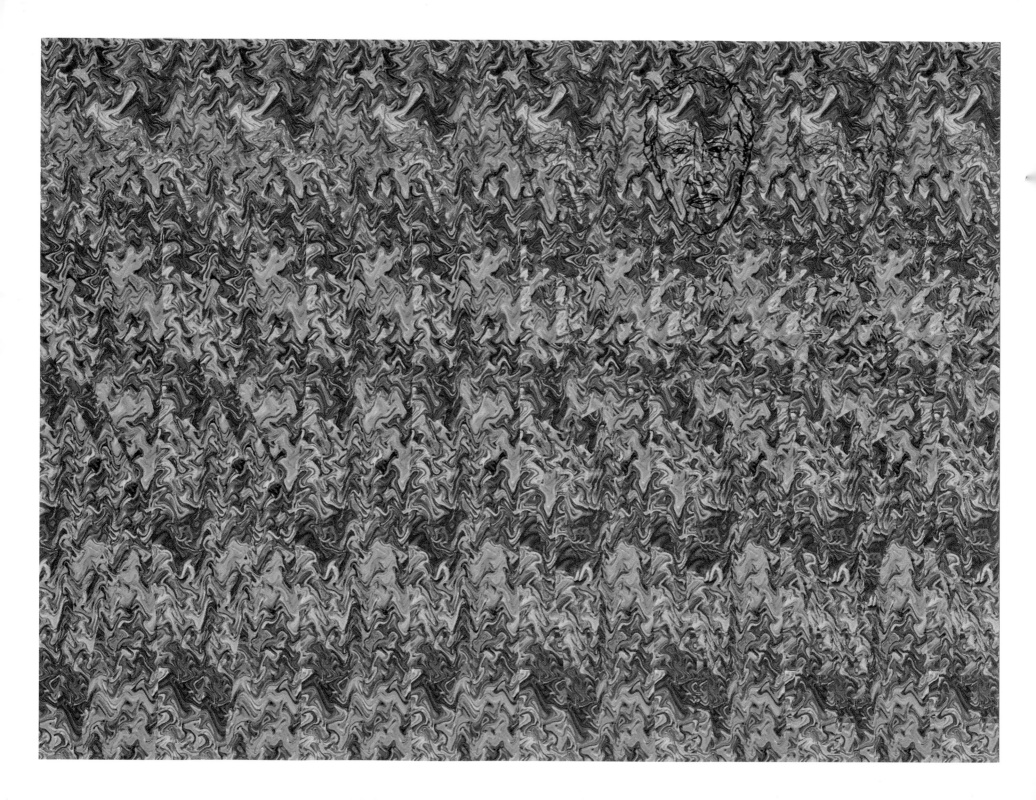

Death at Sea

Cover

Page iv: *Queen's Speed arrives at Dock 23.*

Page 5: *Passengers await permission to leave ship.*

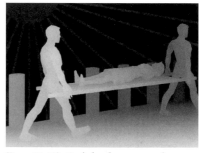

Page 7: *Victim's body removed.*

Page 9: *Steed hands belongings to Bowles.*

Page 15: *Bowles interrogates Steed.*

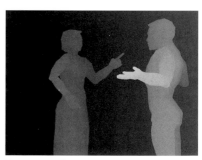

Page 17: *The argument.*

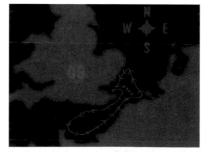

Page 21: *The course of Queen's Speed.*

Page 23: *Clark responds to Bowles's inquiries.*

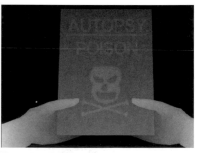

Page 27: *Maggy shares autopsy results with Bowles.*